HEAD OVER HEELS

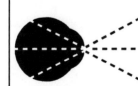

This Large Print Book carries the
Seal of Approval of N.A.V.H.

HEAD OVER HEELS

GAIL SATTLER

THORNDIKE PRESS

An imprint of Thomson Gale, a part of The Thomson Corporation

Detroit • New York • San Francisco • New Haven, Conn. • Waterville, Maine • London

LIBRARY OF CONGRESS CATALOGING-IN-PUBLICATION DATA

Sattler, Gail.
  Head over heels / by Gail Sattler.
    p. cm. — (Thorndike Press large print Christian fiction)
  ISBN-13: 978-0-7862-9506-7 (alk. paper)
  ISBN-10 0-7862-9506-6 (alk. paper)
  I. Title.
PR9199.4.S3575H43 2007
813'.54—dc22   2007000161

Published in 2007 by arrangement with Harlequin Books S.A.

Printed in the United States of America on permanent paper
10 9 8 7 6 5 4 3 2 1

However, as it written, "No eye has seen, no ear has heard, no mind has conceived what God has prepared for those who love him."

— 1 Corinthians 2:9

To Tim, my favorite Web designer

CHAPTER ONE

The cell phone rang from the passenger seat.

Marielle glanced at the display to see that it was one of the youth group members calling. It was also 2:49 p.m., which was a mere four minutes after the students were dismissed for the day. "Not now, Brittany," she muttered as she rammed her foot on the brake pedal to avoid a man who was jaywalking, or rather jay-running, across the street. As soon as the man was out of her path, Marielle picked up speed to the snail's pace of the rest of the downtown traffic.

The phone stopped ringing, but only for as long as it took Brittany to redial.

"This better be important," Marielle grumbled as she turned out of traffic and into the nearest driveway — the entrance leading to an older complex with main-level parking, and a small office building above.

Carefully, she pulled in and stopped, leaving enough room that someone who needed to get into the parking area could pass her. She reached for the still-ringing phone and hit the talk button, but before she could say hello, a deafening *bang* sounded above her head.

Marielle dropped the phone. Instinctively, she ducked and covered her head with her arms. She waited for more — for the car to shake, for the crash of more to hit the car, for a hail of debris to fall around her.

But all was silent.

With her arms still sheltering her head, she peeked up at the ceiling of her car. The center was heavily dented. A groan of stressed metal signified a movement above, and a man's body rolled off the roof and landed limply on the hood.

On impact his eyes fluttered open. For a split second she made eye contact with the man through the windshield. A combination of pain, shock and confusion showed in his face. Then his eyes drifted shut.

Marielle could barely pick up the phone, her hands were shaking so badly. After three jabs she managed to hit the end button on Brittany without speaking to her, then poked out 9-1-1. "A man just landed on the roof of my car!" she yelled to the operator. "I'm at the complex on 5th and Main! Send an ambulance!" Without waiting for a reply, she threw the phone onto the seat.

Marielle pushed the door, but it wouldn't open. Instead of wasting time fighting with it, she scrambled out the window. As her feet touched the ground, people began to gather around her car.

The man lay sprawled on the hood, still on his stomach, not moving. His arms and legs didn't seem to be at odd angles, which Marielle thought was probably a good sign. She didn't see blood gushing from anywhere except his nose. She supposed this was also a good sign.

She could detect labored breathing from the movement of his chest beneath the thin cotton of his shirt.

She focused on controlling her voice to sound as calm as possible, even though her heart was racing and her chest was so tight she could barely breathe. "Can you speak?" she asked, looking into his face, hoping she would be able to tell if he was alert. As she spoke, his eyes opened, but they didn't look right.

Her first impulse was to hold one finger up and see if he could focus on it, not that she would know what to do after that.

The man tensed slightly, as if he wanted to push himself upward but couldn't. His whole body went completely limp, and his head lay heavily on the hood. His eyes turned to her — haunted eyes — but Marielle doubted that he really saw her.

"Why?" he moaned. His eyes rolled back, and he passed out.

Marielle froze. She knew that someone involved in an accident was supposed to keep still and calm until the professionals arrived.

She looked up, as if judging how far he'd fallen would help her figure out what to do.

A woman's head poked out of the third-floor window directly above them.

"Help us!" Marielle called out.

The woman's head disappeared quickly inside without her acknowledging what had happened.

Marielle returned all her attention to the injured man. Trying to be gentle, but firm, Marielle pressed her hands into the center of his back to steady him so he wouldn't have a second fall, this time from the hood of her car onto the cement driveway.

"Does anyone know what to do?" she called out over her shoulder to the people that had gathered around her car. "Is there anyone here with any first-aid training?"

Everyone backed up.

A siren finally sounded in the distance.

Marielle turned back to the man. She could only think of one thing to do until the ambulance arrived, and that was to pray for him.

Just in case he moved, she kept her eyes open while she spoke.

"Dear Lord," she prayed softly, so only the man and God could hear. She looked at his face, a face she knew would haunt her dreams for a long time to come. "Please help this man to live. Please love him and touch him and be with him as You heal whatever injuries he has. Please guide the doctors and nurses, and just make him all better. Amen."

A small group of people ran out of the building. "Russ! Russ!" one of the men called out.

Just then the ambulance arrived. The attendants shooed away everyone but Marielle, instructing her to steady the man while they prepared to move him onto a stretcher. A police car arrived as they secured him to the gurney and slid it into the ambulance.

By the time the ambulance doors closed and the lights and siren went on, quite a large crowd had gathered on the sidewalk, and the traffic on the street had ground to a halt. A crew from the *Daily News* pushed their way through the throng.

The police officer approached her. "Excuse me, I need to take a statement. Is this your vehicle?"

For the first time, Marielle looked at the size of the dent in the roof of her car. "Yes, it is."

"Were there any witnesses?"

"I don't know. I didn't even see anything myself. I was at a dead stop . . ." Marielle's voice trailed off and she shuddered inwardly at her own use of the word *dead.* She didn't want to entertain the possibility. "I pulled out of traffic to answer my cell phone, and that was it. There was this bang and then he rolled off the roof and landed on the hood."

"Did anyone come forward? We need to identify him."

She pointed to a group of people standing beside her car. "Those people came running out of the building. One of them called out the name Russ, but the ambulance got here at the same time." She paused. "Do you think he's going to be okay?"

"I can't say, ma'am. Do you know where he came from?"

Marielle looked up at the three-story building. "I didn't see anything until I heard the bang, and by then it was too late. That's all I know."

The officer tucked the notepad into his

pocket and scribbled a number on a card. "Thank you for your time. Here's the file number — you'll have to report this to your insurance agent. Please call me if you remember anything more."

The second the police officer walked toward the onlookers, a reporter shoved a microphone in her face. "I'm Claudia Firth from the *Daily News.* Do you know if he jumped or if he was pushed?"

"I don't know anything. Just suddenly there was this big bang, and there he was." Marielle trembled at the memory. "If you'll excuse me, I have someplace to be, and I'm late. I think those people know something." She pointed to the bystanders who were now speaking with the officer.

Before the reporter had even lowered the microphone, Marielle turned and hurried to her car.

She gritted her teeth, held her breath, grabbed the handle and pulled, hoping that it could still be opened from the outside, even though she hadn't been able to open it from the inside.

With a *pop* and a groan of stressed metal, the latch gave way. Marielle braced herself to regain her balance after the sudden release of tension, then scrambled in behind the steering wheel. She slammed the door shut, gave it a small push to make sure it would stay closed, and drove away.

Just before she turned out of the parking lot, she glanced in the rearview mirror to where both the police officer and the reporter were speaking to the shrinking crowd.

She wasn't sure what had happened, but she sure wanted to know. . . .

"Hello, Mr. Branson. Just checking up on you again. Are you awake?"

Russ opened one eye and tried to move as little as possible. "Unfortunately, yes," he replied quietly.

"How are you feeling?"

He'd definitely felt better, although right now, he was simply glad to be alive. "I'd feel much better if you could give me something for this headache."

"You know I can't do that yet. We have to get you sitting up so we can go through the routine again. It's time."

"Already?" Russ winced as the nurse helped pull him to a sitting position, taking care not to aggravate his cracked ribs. As she raised the back of the bed, every minute felt like an hour. Finally Russ could lean back again.

"We only have to do this once more in another hour, and then, if everything stays the same, I can leave you alone."

"Good. Don't take it personally, but it's been a long night."

The nurse smiled. "I'm sure it has. Look up. How many fingers this time?"

"Three."

"Good. Now watch my pen."

The nurse shone the flashlight in his eyes while he watched the pen moving around. The beam of light seared into his brain, but he didn't know if that was normal. If it wasn't, he feared they would make him stay.

"You're going pale again. How are you feeling?"

Russ exhaled, not realizing he'd been holding his breath. "Like I've been run over by a truck. Tell me the truth. Are there tire-tread marks on my forehead?"

The nurse cleared her throat and pointed the pen at him. "Mr. Branson . . ."

He almost started to smile, but the movement in his face caused another wave of pain to shoot through his cheeks and up into his broken nose. "I don't want to complain," he said, "but I've still got that splitting headache that just won't go away. And it really hurts when I laugh." Not that he'd actually laughed. Nothing was very funny since he'd regained consciousness. They wouldn't give him any painkillers until he passed the safety time zone that would signify there were no complications to his concussion.

"What time is it?"

Russ sighed, then gasped at the stabbing sensation in his ribs. He cringed and wrapped his arms around himself to support his cracked ribs, but it didn't help. Pushing on the bruises and sore ribs made him see stars.

"The clock is right there behind you on the wall if you want to know," he said.

The nurse tapped the pen on the top of the clipboard. "Quit trying to be funny. We have to do this."

"Okay. It's 5:33 a.m., which means it's almost time that I should be waking up and starting to get ready for work. So if you'll just give me that prescription for the headache, I'll be on my way."

"You know I can't do that. You can leave after forty-eight hours, provided that the doctor okays your release."

"Then how about if you tell me what you've done with my clothes? You won't be back for another hour, right?" He gritted his teeth, trying to block out the pain. If he left now, no one would ever know. Thankfully, because he had no identification with him, they hadn't called his mother or sister.

Soon, he could be back to work like nothing ever happened.

The nurse made a tick mark on the chart, not taking his hint. Then she lowered the clipboard and looked him in the eyes. "We've increased the sarcasm factor. That's good, it means you're alert. Do you know where you are?"

"Let me guess. I'm not in Kansas anymore?"

Her answering scowl almost made Russ laugh, but he knew the pain wouldn't be worth it. "I'm in Wakeville, Washington, at Memorial Hospital, and unless you moved me when I wasn't watching, I'm in the South Wing, room 347, bed C."

"More sarcasm." She made another tick mark on his chart and smiled sweetly at him. "You're doing fine. I'll be back in an hour and we'll do this again for the last time. Then the doctor will see you. If there are no changes, he'll give you that prescription, and you can rest until tomorrow night when we can let you go home. I'll lower the bed again now, and you can try to get some sleep."

"Oh, sure," he grumbled. The pain of the headache and the jabbing ache in his lungs every time he inhaled didn't allow him to relax, never mind actually sleep. Besides, it was morning. He'd never been able to sleep in daylight no matter how tired he was. His current level of discomfort and noise of the hospital as it woke up would make sleep an impossibility. The only way he would fall asleep would be in the familiarity of his own bed — and heavily medicated.

"Then would you like to read the morning newspaper? I can hear the cart coming down the hall."

Russ opened his mouth, about to ask what day it was, but fortunately thought better of it, just in case Nurse Drill Sergeant thought it was a bad sign. Yesterday, the day of his accident, had been Monday. He'd been unconscious only a few hours, so today must be Tuesday.

"I can't buy a paper because I don't have any money. My wallet never made it here. Remember?" Also, as much as he did want to read the morning paper, he feared that straining to see the small print would make his headache worse.

The nurse nodded. "You're right, I remember now. But it's okay, because you have a visitor. Keep it under twenty minutes, please."

A woman now stood in the doorway. "Hello? Russ? Can I come in?" Without waiting for a reply, she walked in as the nurse walked out.

Russ's head swam. He didn't recognize her.

He knew he'd received quite a blow to the head, not to mention the rest of his body. But now, rather than simply being annoyed with his current condition, he experienced a touch of panic. Was he in worse condition than the nursing staff had led him to believe?

The last thing he could remember was sitting at his desk, working, fighting with the new program he was trying to install on his computer. The next thing he remembered was waking up in the hospital and a doctor rushing over to him. They had told him it was within normal parameters that he couldn't remember the details of the fall or the trauma leading up to it, but if he'd sustained a permanent brain injury, he didn't know if he could deal with that.

The woman pulled a chair to the side of the bed and lowered herself into it without taking her eyes off him. "How are you feeling?"

He stared into her face, struggling for recall. She appeared to be a couple of years younger than him, in her late twenties. Her hair was in a blunt cut, medium brown and sporting a streak of bright red on one side

— something he definitely should have remembered. Her green eyes bordered on gray, and they were bright and alert, and curious, fixed on his face — compelling him to maintain that eye contact rather than check her out.

When she'd walked into the room he'd seen that she had a slender build, yet when studying her face, he thought she had rather round cheeks. She was pretty, despite the strange hair color. She wore a little makeup, just enough to highlight full lips, along with a bit of mascara that added length to the longest eyelashes he'd ever seen.

She appeared to know him, but he didn't remember her.

"I — I'm sorry," he stammered. "Do I know you?"

"Technically, we've met before, but I can't blame you for not remembering me." She dug through her purse and placed his wallet on the small table beside the bed. "I found this stuck in the slot where the windshield wipers are when I got home last night. I guess it got stuck there when you fell. I hope you don't mind that I looked inside. I had to know your name so they would let me in. My name is Marielle McGee, and that was my car you landed on."

His vision lost focus as he struggled to

remember details. All he knew was what the nurses had told him — that he'd fallen out a window and, instead of landing on the hard cement, he'd landed on a car, which had made the landing less serious than it might have been. While short-term memory loss was common for the injury he'd sustained, it still worried him.

"I don't know what to say. You probably saved my life."

"Oh . . . Well . . . Speaking of that, do you want to talk about it? I'm a good listener."

"It's okay," he said as he brushed his index finger over the bandage that covered his nose. "I've been told that no permanent damage was done."

Her tone softened. "Don't worry. I'm a volunteer counselor at my church. Sometimes it's easier to talk to a stranger about things like this."

"About things like . . . what?"

"Problems. Depression. Despondency. Things that would drive a person to acts of desperation."

"Desperation?" The pain in his head worsened as he realized what she meant. "Please don't worry. I don't remember what happened, but I'm not suicidal. My life is good. I have a good job, a nice home, and I can assure you that I didn't do anything that drastic because of a broken heart. I've been much too busy to get involved in a relationship —"

His voice caught. Thinking of work, a shadow of a memory flashed through his mind. For some reason, he'd gotten up and walked to the window. He couldn't remember why. But all jokes aside, he knew that he wouldn't kill himself out of frustration with his computer. Besides, statistically, jumping out of a window wasn't usually fatal unless it was the seventh story or higher.

"Do you believe in God, Russ?"

"Yes, of course I do."

"I mean as more than just the Creator of the universe. Do you believe in God, who loves all the children He's created, including you?"

"Yeah." He just hadn't been to church lately. Actually, he hadn't been to church for a long time. On a few occasions, he'd weakened and gone back, but he didn't know why. Going to church or not going to church didn't make any difference. Nothing got better, nothing changed. He'd struggled and worked hard, and he had been faithful, but God hadn't given him any breaks in his youth, and God didn't give him any breaks now. God made him work, and work hard for everything he had. It seemed God never considered his debt repaid.

He cleared his throat. "Please don't worry. I'm fine. In fact, I'm anxious to get back to work. I'm a Web designer, and I'm in the middle of designing a big interactive Web site for an important client."

"Oh." She paused, then shuffled something in her hand. "It's just that, well, the newspaper . . ." Her voice trailed off.

"The newspaper?"

"The newspaper is saying something very different than what you're telling me right now."

Russ gulped. "You mean there was a reporter there?"

Marielle nodded. "Yes. And it appears they've done quite a bit of research, first on the history and infrastructure of the old building, and also . . . on you."

She held the newspaper out to him, and Russ's hand trembled as he accepted it. Was it possible the newspaper knew more about what had happened than he did?

CHAPTER TWO

Marielle watched Russ's eyes widen, then squeeze shut after he read the front-page headline: Near Death at Downtown Office.

"I don't believe this. . . ." He opened his eyes and continued reading. "I'm not nearly dead. It was only the third floor! And they're being really vague about whether I jumped or fell. I don't remember what happened, but I certainly didn't jump." He reached up to touch the bridge of his nose, but stopped when his fingers brushed the bandage. "They even quoted a few people I work with as saying they didn't know what happened." He lowered the paper to his lap. "In one sentence the reporter insinuated that I jumped, and then in the next says it's unconfirmed. How can they print this?"

Marielle looked into his face. All the training and courses she'd taken for her position as volunteer counselor at her church told her that he was sincere. He really hadn't jumped, and she'd been worried about him for nothing. It was simply an accident.

"Because sensationalism sells, I guess."

"I suppose. The truth is often boring."

A silence hung between them for a few minutes.

"I guess you're here to make arrangements for your car. I probably left a pretty big dent. May I see your estimate?"

Marielle felt her cheeks heat up. "I haven't got an estimate yet. I was busy last night, and I'm on my way to work right now. I actually came just to see how you were, and to return your wallet. I had better get going or I'm going to be late."

"Let me give you my phone number, then, and call me as soon as you know. Would you give me your phone number, too?"

"Sure."

"I want you to know that if you hadn't been there, I would have been seriously injured, maybe even permanently disabled. I know your car was damaged. I don't want to be more of an inconvenience to you than I've already been. If you go to your insurance agent and this raises your rates for the next few years, I want to know, and I'd like to pay the difference."

Marielle stood and smiled. "Thanks. That's really nice of you."

She turned to go, but she'd only taken one step when a man of average build and height who looked to be in his mid-forties appeared in the doorway. When he saw her standing beside the bed, he quickly turned his head to check the number on the door, then continued inside. His polite smile, easy demeanor and friendly brown eyes immediately made Marielle feel relaxed.

When he turned to Russ his smile faltered, but he recovered quickly. "Hi, Russ. You've looked better."

"Thanks. I needed to hear that. I've felt better, too. Grant, this is, uh, Mary Ellen, is it?"

"You're close. It's Marielle. But don't worry about it. It happens all the time."

"I'm so sorry. Grant, this is Marielle, the woman whose car I landed on. Marielle, this is Grant, my boss."

Grant immediately grasped her hand. "I'm so glad to meet you. I asked about you when the ruckus died down, but no one knew who you were, or where you came from. You were like Cinderella, disappearing at the stroke of midnight. You were in the paper with your statement — but then things got so busy. And the calls . . ."

Marielle smiled sympathetically. "I've had lots of questions about yesterday, too."

"I want to do something to make it up to you. After all, Russ is my best employee. But now that we're face to face, I wish I knew what to suggest."

"I was simply put in the right place at the right time. If you have to thank someone, then thank Brittany. It was because of her that I had to park to answer my cell phone. Now, if you'll excuse me, I have to get to work. It was nice meeting you both."

Russ and Grant looked up at the clock on the wall. "It's not even six o'clock," Russ said. "You have a very early start to your day. What do you do?"

"It's just an office job. I work in accounting. I start at six and get off at two-thirty. But I start early because I go someplace else afterward."

"You mean you have a second job?"

Marielle froze. *Second job? Not anymore.*

She shuffled her purse under her arm, pretending she needed to concentrate on it so that she didn't have to look at the two men while she spoke. "It's not a job. I volunteer for a youth program that teaches underprivileged kids computer skills so they'll know how to use computers for more than just memorizing the cheat codes from the latest online games."

Grant nodded. "Well, good luck, and it

was nice meeting you. I hope we can . . ." Grant's voice trailed off.

Before Marielle could walk away, he wrapped his fingers around her arm, preventing her from leaving. "Wait. If you won't take anything personally for what you did, can I make a donation to your organization?"

Marielle looked up at the clock again. "That would be great. We've had a bunch of new members join the group. We need to get more equipment and there's never enough money."

"You know, I've been thinking of upgrading some of my office's computers. Instead of trading them in, how about if I donate them to your group? It sounds like you could really use them. Let me give you my card so we can set up an appointment."

Marielle wanted to be on time, but at the mention of the donation, she knew her boss at her day job would excuse her for being a few minutes late. At times Marielle brought in some of the older and more promising teens for summer relief work or other odd jobs at her company. More computers at the youth center meant that down the line she could bring in more experienced helpers — a definite bonus for her boss.

She smiled. "That would be great."

"Think of this as my way of making things up to you." Grant turned to Russ as he reached into his back pocket. "I think the first computer that we'll replace will be yours."

Russ grinned in response. "I won't argue with that. When I get back to work, I'll make sure all my backups are current."

Grant froze, his hand resting on his pocket. "You're *not* coming back to work anytime soon. You need some time off."

"I thought you came here to take me back to work, since I don't have my car here."

"I came to check on you, then tomorrow I'll return to drive you home — and leave you there."

"But what about that project?"

The two men stared at each other as if she weren't there, which she wished were true. She wanted Grant's card, but she needed to get to her own job.

Grant's hand remained motionless on his back pocket as he spoke. "You're my best employee, Russ, but you work too much. Everyone needs some time off, and you're taking yours *now.*"

"I can't just sit at home and stare at the walls all day, knowing my work is piling up. I'll go insane."

"Then, tell you what. If you're really up

to it, why don't you help the nice young lady out at the youth center? Help her make room for the new computers — starting with yours."

"But . . ."

Marielle had to interrupt. "Excuse me. I hate to be rude but I really have to get to work. If you can give me your card, I'll call you later today."

"Of course. Sorry." Grant pulled his wallet out, removed the card and handed it to her. "Call me anytime."

"I will. Thanks."

"Wait. You didn't give me your card."

"I don't have cards. But don't worry, I'll call you."

Marielle quickly left the room, but as she walked out she heard Grant say, "Marielle, huh? Interesting name."

Marielle's feet skidded to a halt.

"Yeah," Russ replied. "It's different."

"This is just like how she left yesterday." A trace of laughter colored Grant's voice. "Except you sure don't look like our Cinderella's Prince Charming with your face like that. Are you ever going to be handsome again?" Grant broke out into a full laugh.

"Forget it," Russ grumbled, with no trace of amusement in his voice. "I'm not her

Prince Charming, and I'm not *going* to be her Prince Charming. I know what you're thinking, and I'm not interested."

Marielle gulped air, along with a good portion of her pride, as she turned around and hurried out.

While she definitely wasn't looking for another Prince Charming, it hurt to be so easily brushed off. *Again.* Maybe Michael — the man she had thought was her Prince Charming — was right, and the problem really was her, after all.

But this time, instead of dwelling over her hurt, Marielle chose to be happy that she was getting more computers for the youth center. That was all that mattered in her life right now. It might have been a rather unpleasant way to get them, but God had provided an opportunity to help a bunch of kids who needed more than their parents could give them in order to have a brighter future. It was her duty to follow through — whatever Prince Not-So-Charming felt about her.

For now, she had more important things to do than worry about him.

CHAPTER THREE

By the time Russ made it up the first flight
of stairs on the way to his third-floor office
he knew he'd made a mistake, but it was
too late to turn back. Usually he enjoyed
the exercise. Today, he would have given
nearly anything for the choice of an elevator
— something the older building where his
office was located didn't have. Every step
up jarred his ribs, but if he took any more
painkillers, he wouldn't be able to think
straight or drive safely.

He told himself that he had a good reason
for what he was doing. The sooner he could
clear out his old computer, the sooner he
could get a new one and get back to work.
Even though it was midafternoon, that still
gave him a couple of hours to catch up on
what he'd missed with Tyler, his assistant,
and then after everyone left, Russ would
have the office to himself to work in peace
and quiet. Then he didn't have to worry that

anyone would watch him suffer while he finished constructing the database and doing more work on the programming for Byron's interactive Web site, which was his current project.

He doubted he could ever repay his debt to Marielle, but now he had one more thing for which he owed her. First she had been responsible for saving his life, and now she was responsible for his getting a new computer.

Russ didn't like owing debts. He'd had enough of debts. The only debts he wanted to have were his mortgage and his car payments — manageable debts and nothing else.

By the time his hand touched the doorknob to the main office on the third floor, his chest hurt so much he was dizzy. He wanted to walk into the office looking like he was fine and justified in coming back to work, so he leaned against the wall until he could regain his bearings and prepare himself to face his workmates.

When he finally opened the door and entered the main office, everyone stopped their activity and stared at him. He smiled weakly as he walked past Brenda, the receptionist. She stood, and good manners dictated that he stop.

"Russ? What are you doing here? How are you feeling?"

Automatically he raised one hand to touch the bandage covering the bridge of his nose. He wrapped his other arm around his rib cage, just in case the support bandage covering his chest showed through his shirt. "I'm feeling better than I look. Where's Grant?"

"He's in your office," replied Tyler. "With someone."

"Good." Grant was usually very prompt, and today was no exception. Already, Grant had the technician in there to discuss their needs for the new system.

Recovered from the climb and full of ideas, Russ opened the door to his private office and stepped inside.

"Hey, Grant! This is . . ." His smile faltered. "Marielle? What are you doing here?"

She turned around and smiled so brightly she nearly glowed.

"I was on my way to the youth center, so I thought I'd stop in and have a look at the computers."

He glanced around the room. "Where's the tech?"

Grant shook his head. "He was busy today. He'll be here tomorrow morning. By

36

the way, what are you doing here? I thought you were taking the week off."

"There are a few things I need to take care of, and I also thought I'd clear out my old computer. I always keep backups, but there is some other stuff I have to do."

"You'll be able to clear your data quickly, right?"

"You bet. I like to have everything organized."

"Then I have an idea. Marielle is so excited — since you're here, I think it would be a nice gesture to give her the first computer to take now. That would be yours."

"Now?" He'd barely survived the trip up the stairs. He'd fully intended to sit at his desk for the last few hours of the day to work on his current project. If all he had to do was clear everything he'd already backed up the day of the accident, he would only have a few minutes' worth of work.

He'd nearly killed himself to get into the office. He wanted to make being there worth the effort.

Grant studied him. "Did you ask your doctor about the wisdom of coming to work today?"

Russ kept his mouth shut. He knew what his doctor would have said, and Russ thought otherwise.

Marielle checked her watch. "I have to be at the youth center to open up. I'm so sorry. I know it always seems I don't have time to chat, but I must go."

Grant raised one palm. "Wait. Russ, if you're itching to do something, why don't you go to the youth center with Marielle? I've dug up some old versions of different graphics programs we've bought over the years. I think I'll donate those, too. Can you go through the box, grab what you think would be best, and we'll meet you at the car?"

Grant turned back to Marielle, then stopped and looked back at Russ. "After that, go home and don't come back to the office until next week."

"Uh, sure . . . But that will leave you shorthanded. And I haven't seen Jessie, either. Where is she, by the way? I thought she was supposed to be in." Russ turned to Marielle. "Jessie is a contract employee who was working on a special project with me."

Grant nodded. "I tried to call, but all I got was her voice mail. It's strange that she didn't come in, but then, I'm not paying her by the hour, so she can work anywhere she wants, just so she meets her deadlines."

Russ turned back to Grant. "That may be so, but we were at a point where we had to work on this phase together, from here, because you don't have multiple licenses for the programs we need right now." He turned back to Marielle and pointed to Grant's office. "The program we need is on the server in Grant's office. We have the computers in the office linked, but we can't access it remotely. The rest of the work has to be done here, and we're on that tight deadline for Byron."

Grant frowned. "Speaking of our client, he e-mailed me earlier today asking me to put a temporary hold on everything."

Russ spun toward his boss so fast his ribs ached. "I don't understand. What happened?"

"I don't know. But since the project is set back, this is a really good time for you to take the computer to the youth center before another big project comes up."

"I guess." Before he could say any more, a few of the men from the office appeared, and within minutes, all the components of his computer were gone.

He made his selection of program CD-ROMs, and then made his way downstairs. Fortunately the trip down was easier than the trip up, and he soon joined Grant and Marielle on the ground level. When they saw him, the conversation stopped until he was at Grant's side.

"I know you have other things to do," Grant said, "but I'm not kidding when I say I don't want you to get any ideas about coming back to work too soon. Take tomorrow and sleep in, and if you're feeling restless, you can go straight to the youth center in the afternoon and meet Marielle there to show her how to use the programs. In fact, I want you to take Friday off, too. That way you can have more time to teach her." He turned to Marielle. "Most of those programs have a help file, so you'll be fine after he walks you through everything."

"But . . ." Russ knew what Grant was trying to do. Doing something for a charity was good publicity. Russ would rather have worked on other projects, but hopefully a couple of additional days off wouldn't matter. If this was how Grant wanted him to help, so be it. "Okay," he sighed. "I can do that."

"Good. Have fun."

Russ gritted his teeth. *Fun* wasn't going to happen. Spending time in a charity organization with a bunch of underprivileged teenaged hoodlums was the last thing he wanted to do.

He'd spent all of his growing-up years in that environment. The grueling poverty. The constant struggles. The pressure to look cool while deep inside he felt helpless and desperate to escape. He'd worked long and hard to get out. He'd humbled himself and swallowed his pride and done everything his boss at the time had asked, even though his friends had looked down on him and called him weak and a pushover, and had ridiculed him. At that time all he had was his personal honor, and he believed God was on his side. He put in some very long hours and worked hard and did his best to please his employers — doing all the dirty work no one else would do, and taking his business courses at night school. When it came time to select the one person who could move out of the factory and into a supervisory position, Russ got the job, and the raise that went with it, and later, a good reference for a better job out of that neighborhood. At that point, he finally had a future, even with all his debts. It had taken until he was twenty-five, but he'd moved on and was out of the slums, never to sink to that level again.

Except that Grant had just told him to go back.

Russ could feel the pangs of his ulcer acting up, but he told himself that helping Marielle was a way to earn brownie points toward the promotion he so desperately wanted.

"Okay. I'll do it. Let's go."

He got into his car and followed Marielle to the back of an old church building in a less-than-upscale area of the city.

As soon as Marielle got out of her car, four teenage boys wearing leather jackets and ripped jeans joined her. She pointed to the computer in the back seat. "Look what we've got!" she said as she unlocked the door.

The boys expressed their pleasure in current jargon that Russ made no attempt to follow, and carried everything into the building.

Russ trailed behind them through a large doorway, down a flight of stairs and into a large well-lit room with a dull tile floor. A few tables lined the far wall, and in each corner was a shelf in need of repair. An old wooden desk, piled with papers and books sat to the side of the door.

Russ turned to Marielle. "Is there always someone here waiting for you?"

She nodded. "I'm usually here a little sooner than this. I time it so I can arrive not long after they get off school. Many of them need a place that's not an empty house. They're all old enough to be left home alone, but that doesn't mean it's best."

Russ stared at her. At that age, every day he'd gone home to an empty apartment and often he'd ended up doing things he shouldn't have been doing. He'd almost started on a downward spiral like all his friends, but at the last minute had realized that he had to do something right that second if he wanted to escape the trap and make something out of his life.

By the time he realized what would happen if he didn't get his act together, it had still been too late to do what he really wanted, which was get a scholarship for university. He'd already messed up his grades too much by focusing on his immediate needs: his minimum-wage job and trying to fit in with those he thought were his friends, instead of studying. Also, by then he had a reputation to live up to — or to live down to.

Still, he'd done more than most of his friends. He was the first to have a job and stick with it. He made up his mind to do what it took to pass, and actually graduated from high school, got a student loan and went on to business college.

Marielle smiled at him, breaking him out of his memories.

"Everyone else will be here soon. We'd better get started."

Marielle stood back to watch the flurry. Russ had picked a table in the corner of the room and was setting up the computer. As she'd expected, the boys gathered around him, asking a million questions while the girls stayed with Marielle watching from across the room.

"I'll bet he'll be a real hottie when he gets that thing off his face," a female voice whispered behind Marielle, then broke into giggles. "And if he has a bump on his nose from it being broken, that's so sexy."

Marielle turned around to see Brittany. Today, Brittany was wearing her trendy clothes way too tight, and again in Marielle's opinion, she was wearing too much makeup for a sixteen-year-old girl.

"Forget it, Brittany. I'm not interested."

Brittany giggled again. "Why not? He's so handsome, and he seems smart, too."

"Being smart isn't everything," Marielle replied. And she'd certainly had it with handsome.

She'd seen enough of Russ to know what he was really about, and she knew the type well. She'd seen the same traits in Michael. At first, she'd admired him, and before long, she'd fallen in love. He was dedicated, and seemed to have admirable goals. He had promised to work hard at his career to provide a good future for both of them. He had had big plans and he aimed high. At first she'd helped — even supported him while he worked part time and went to college part time, all in order to achieve those goals that were supposed to benefit them as a couple. She'd almost driven herself to exhaustion to do it, because she loved him.

But still, nothing was good enough. When she said she needed some downtime to see her friends and church family, whom she'd been ignoring for Michael, he told her it wasn't the right time. Even though he worked long hours, Michael wasn't content with what they had, and he always had to work harder to get more. No matter how much money he made, nothing would satisfy him, he always wanted bigger and better and more expensive. First, he wanted a bigger house and a better new car — for both of them, he claimed. But because they weren't married, *he* was the one living in the house, and *he* was the one driving the expensive new car. Soon he began to forsake everything but activities that could earn him more money to get an even bigger house and an even better car.

And then, three days before what was supposed to be their wedding day, Michael called it off, leaving her to phone everyone and cancel. Within a few hours of announcing this, he ran off with a woman he worked with — a woman who also wanted the biggest and best, and the latest and the greatest out of life, a woman who had the very college education that Marielle had given up to work two jobs so that Michael could go to college instead. Elaine was exactly like Michael, in feminine form.

Marielle vowed she would never go through that again. Maybe one day she might be able to take a chance and open her heart, but when she did, it wouldn't be to a man who was driven to work until he nearly dropped, but to someone who could be content with what God had given him.

As she watched Russ boot up the computer after he had everything connected, she noted that *especially* included a man so obsessed with work that he was back on the job without taking sufficient time to recuperate after a three-story fall.

But for now, Russ was an answer to one particular prayer. The center needed more computers. She'd had such success with her outreach ministry in the community that she had doubled the anticipated number of regular attendees in her ragtag group. God had provided for her needs, so she would do whatever was necessary to help the teens who needed it.

One of the boys smacked Russ on the back as the prompt showing that the first program had been successfully installed flashed on the screen. The pain of the impact showed clearly on Russ's face.

Marielle cringed on his behalf. Instead of working, Russ should have been in bed. Resting. Healing.

His priorities were all wrong. It didn't take a rocket scientist to see that he wasn't here because of a burning need to help the underprivileged teens. He was only here because his boss had told him to come, and as a step toward getting a new computer for himself faster.

She wasn't impressed.

A male voice broke into her thoughts. "Have you seen all these programs?"

She spun around to see Jason, her most promising member, sitting on the floor picking through the boxes.

Jason held up one of the program CDs. "Look at this graphics program! Most people have to take a course for it. And we're getting it for free!"

"Course?" Marielle said. "What kind of

course?"

Jason stood. "A couple of the kids in my physics class are taking it at night. It's four weeks, and it's too expensive for my mom to pay for." He glanced over at Russ. "Will he be able to teach this to us?"

"I think he's going to teach it to me tomorrow, and then I'm going to teach it to all of you."

Jason blinked. "You're kidding. Right?"

Marielle watched Russ push the chair back and stand.

"That's it for tonight," he said. "But I'll be back tomorrow to show you how to work some of these programs."

Jason edged closer to Marielle. "It's taking Josh and Sara four weeks to learn that one."

Marielle gulped. "I'm sure it won't take me that long." She hoped . . .

CHAPTER FOUR

Marielle pulled into the church parking lot earlier than usual, but she was still too late. Another vehicle was parked in the otherwise empty lot. A shiny new SUV, something far more expensive than any of the other cars that would have been parked in this neighborhood.

She parked beside it, noting, as she got out and walked past, the blinking red security light, as well as the locking bar mechanism bolted to the steering wheel.

She almost felt like giving it a shove, just to see what happened. Almost.

Russ stood waiting for her at the basement door.

"You could have gone in through the front. I told Pastor Tom you were coming and what you looked like."

"That's okay. I didn't want to start until some of the kids were here anyway."

Marielle lowered her voice in case one of

them came up behind her. "Don't *ever* call them kids. They're at that sensitive point where they're too old to be kids, but not old enough to be young adults. Some of them have to make life-changing decisions, right now or soon, and I'm trying to guide them to make the right ones. I can't do anything to jeopardize what they're doing here."

She wondered if it was her imagination, but she thought he cringed at her censure.

"I'm sorry. You're right."

She sighed. "I'm sorry, too. I shouldn't have snapped at you. Let's go inside."

She began the process of unlocking the door while he stood behind her.

"I thought you said the pastor was here."

"He is here," she replied. "Sometimes his wife drops him off when she needs the car."

She couldn't help but sneak a glance at him over her shoulder. Just as she had suspected, he was checking out the old building.

What he saw wasn't exactly pristine. The building had probably been impressive in its day, but now it was badly in need of repair. The church board had decided the pastor needed the money to live on more than they needed the building to look nice. The old stone front definitely could stand to be sandblasted, which they couldn't afford. But because of a couple of volunteers, the brightly colored stained-glass windows on either side of the steeple were always washed and bright.

Yet still some of those beautiful windows needed work. A few of the glass pieces were scratched from vandals throwing stones, and the sills and edges were showing deterioration due to weather over the years.

The mechanism used to ring the old bell inside the tower hadn't been functional for years, but because so many of the nearby residents didn't attend church, the community had blocked all efforts the church board made to city council for funding to restore it as a heritage site.

The cement steps in the front had been chipped and broken in places, but that had been relatively easy for members of the congregation to repair, although the new cement didn't match the original color or texture. The most important thing, though, was that the steps were safe. They were the only part of the building that met current earthquake standards. Still, Marielle thought the building looked stately, and respected it for its history.

Where they were now entering, however, wasn't so regal. Like the rest of the humble neighborhood, the back of the church, where no one of importance usually ventured, wasn't kept up. The windows were too high to be reached with ease — except by a special extended ladder — so they weren't washed, and no one cared about the lower windows leading to the basement. The original back door had been made of wood, but many years before Marielle started to attend that church, vandals had damaged it beyond repair. Now a stark metal door, layered with different colors of paint to cover graffiti, took its place.

Just as Marielle pushed the big door open, Russ turned and looked at her car. "Are you going to get that roof fixed soon? I'd like to take care of it."

"I don't have time during the week. It will have to wait until the weekend. One of the parents of one of my boys works at an auto body shop. He said he'll give me a good deal."

"Okay."

Once inside, Marielle locked her purse inside her desk and joined Russ at his former computer. "What do you have to do to it today?"

He turned in the chair in which he had seated himself, and she noticed that he winced with the movement.

"Not a lot. Today I'll install the rest of the programs I brought, and then I'll show you and everyone else how to use them."

"I thought I should let you know, I don't think I'm as good with computers as your boss thinks I am. My being here has more to do with my availability and willingness to do the job than my programming skills."

"Apparently, I'll be back tomorrow, but if you need more help we could get together on the weekend and I can give you a better tutorial."

She had plans for the weekend with a girlfriend, but Marielle was almost sure that Lorraine wouldn't mind. Lorraine understood what she was doing with the teen outreach program, even if she didn't have time to participate herself. "That's a great idea, thanks."

Right on schedule, the teens began to arrive, starting with Jason, who was always the first. Marielle waited for fifteen minutes, and when all her core group was accounted for, Russ began installing the first program, showing everyone where to find the tutorials and help files.

This time, instead of standing back, Marielle stayed close by, also watching and learning. She wasn't confident that she would be of much help if anyone needed anything, but she wanted to do her best when the time came.

"Hello? Russ? Are you in here?"

All heads turned toward the door to watch Russ's boss enter.

"Grant? What are you doing here?"

Grant smiled. "I wanted to see the place, so I decided this would be a good time to bring a few more computers."

"Now? You brought them already?"

Grant made eye contact with some of the bigger boys. "Yup. Four more are in my car. Who is going to help carry them inside?"

The teens made a beeline for the exit. The boys dashed outside after Grant; the girls stopped at the doorway to watch, whispered among themselves, then walked outside, too.

Which left Marielle and Russ alone in the room.

Russ ran his fingers through his hair as he stared at the empty doorway. "I didn't expect this. I guess I won't be installing the programs today." He turned back to her. "The trouble is that I don't know what's been done and if they're ready."

The boys appeared through the door one by one, like a row of ants, each carrying either a monitor or a tower, the girls each carrying a keyboard and a mouse or bundles of cables. Grant brought up the rear, empty-handed. "That's it for today," he said. "Let's get started getting everything hooked up."

Marielle, Russ, Grant, and the teens began the job of connecting the cables and positioning the computers on the desks.

"Do I assume that my computer as well as these other ones have now been replaced at the office?" Russ asked as he untangled cable.

Grant nodded as he tightened a connection. "Yes. We got half today, the other half will be coming Monday. But don't try to sneak in tomorrow. There's nothing urgent happening at the office anyway. Jessie finally called in sick yesterday afternoon, and today she didn't show up."

Russ crossed his arms over his chest, taking in a deep breath when he pressed his arms against his ribs, confirming to Marielle, as if she needed it, that Russ really wasn't in any shape to be going back to work.

"That's odd," Russ said. He turned to Marielle. "Jessie works for us on contract, so she doesn't get paid for sick time. She tends to come to work when she's sick, even if she should have stayed in bed." He turned back to Grant. "Jessie must be really sick to stay home. Did she say what was wrong?"

"Actually, no. Yesterday she left a message

on my voice mail, and she spoke really quickly. I tried calling her back, but I got *her* voice mail. I had expected her to call again today if she wasn't going to be in. . . ." Grant shrugged. "It's not like her not to check in. I tried calling her again after the tech called, but I got her voice mail again. Monday we'll be busy setting up the second set of new computers. That means you don't have to be there. I'm not sure about Jessie. We'll have to wait for her to call me back."

Russ didn't respond, but as Marielle watched, his face paled.

She leaned toward him. "Russ? What's wrong?"

He lowered his head and pressed his fingers into his temples. "I thought I was over this headache, but I can't seem to shake it."

Grant stood, hovering as Russ remained seated. "Which is another reason you need to take some time off. I did a little research yesterday, and recurring headaches is a common side effect of a serious concussion. Consider yourself off for a week on medical leave. The accident happened on Monday, so you're off the rest of the week."

"But —"

Grant raised one hand to prevent Russ from arguing. "I mean it. I've been watching you work your tail off every day, and I don't know offhand how much vacation time I owe you, all I know is that it's a lot. You say you can't remember what happened, but I wonder if part of the reason you feel like that is that you're overstressed. I don't want you coming in to the office until next week, and until then I want you to only spend a couple of hours a day here *if* you feel up to it, and that's it. Now if you'll excuse me, I have to take my son to a ball game tonight. You can handle it from here, right?"

Grant apparently didn't expect a response, because he didn't wait for one. Marielle wanted to call out after him that his expectations could have been one of the reasons Russ was overworked and overstressed, but she remained silent. It wasn't any of her business.

Russ leaned to one side, reached into his pocket and pulled out a couple of white pills. "Where can I get some water? The doctor said to take these if the headache came back, and wow, has it ever come back."

"There's a fountain over there, by the washrooms."

Russ stood, then sank back into the chair. "I can't take these. I have to drive home later." He returned the pills to his pocket, then returned his attention to the computer as he began the process of putting it back together. The tightness in his face showed how he was trying to fight the pain.

"You don't have to do this. It can wait until tomorrow."

He winced as he lowered himself to his hands and knees. "I'd rather do it now and get it over with," he said as he crawled under the desk. She heard a sharp intake of breath as he leaned all the way to the back to connect the keyboard to the tower. "Besides, I'd rather not drive in traffic with a headache like this. It will pass."

He backed out slowly, then returned to the chair. His face was even paler than it had been earlier.

"Would you like to lie down for a few minutes? I'm not exactly sure what to do with the program, but I can follow the prompts and call if something happens."

"I'm fine," he said, although the way his hands were shaking told her otherwise.

"You still don't remember what happened that day, do you?"

He stopped his work and turned to her. "No, I don't. I just keep seeing Jessie's face, almost like in a fog, not clear but I know it's her. Everything else is blank. I remember sitting at my desk, and getting up for some reason that keeps evading me, and then the next thing I remember is waking up in the hospital with the nurses and a doctor hovering over me. The doctor told me that holes in a person's memory sometimes happen and just to give it time, but that's easier said than done. It bothers me."

"I can only imagine." As much as she didn't think too highly of his overwork ethics, she didn't want him to suffer. Memories of his face and his expression as he lay on the hood of her car still haunted her. A number of days had passed already, and she knew he was fine — or at least better than the alternative.

He squeezed his eyes shut and sighed. "I don't even know why I'm telling you this."

Marielle smiled. "I think it's because I have an honest face." Aside from the fact that she liked helping people, all her life, people had found her easy to talk to, which made a difference in her work as a volunteer counselor — especially with the youths. They trusted her because she did her best, without being pushy, to help the youths take a straight path as they chose the direction they would go into adulthood. Russ was an adult, but regardless of how she personally felt about someone who was a chronic workaholic, he was there in front of her. If he needed someone in a difficult time, she would do the same for him as she would for anyone else.

"Yes, you do," he said, smiling, as he reached for a loose mouse.

"If you want, I can pray with you about it. I believe in miracles, and I believe that you being here is a miracle in itself."

"No thanks," he muttered. "I've used up my quota of miracles."

Marielle's breath caught. "Surely you don't believe that."

He held out one hand. "Can you pass me that cable over there?"

She stared at him, and when nothing more was said, she handed him the cable. He couldn't have been more clear about not wanting to talk — or pray — if he'd slammed a door in her face.

He made his way down the row of computers, one by one, reinstalling operating systems. Each time he left a chair, one of the youths slid in to finish off the process or report on the progress.

As he worked, he chatted pleasantly with all the youths, although it was quickly apparent that the boys were interested in the computers, and most of the girls were interested in Russ.

Six o'clock came before Marielle even realized it. "That was the fastest three hours I've ever spent here," she said, looking up at the clock on the wall.

"Is that how long you run the drop-in? Three hours every day?"

"Yes. It's meant to be a place for them to go after school. We also run on Friday evenings, so they won't get into trouble."

"You come here Friday night, too?"

"Yes. We try to get volunteers to help, but most of the time it's just me. I wish we could run the center on Saturday, but I just can't do it all by myself and we can't get enough people to commit. The Sunday school uses this room on Sunday morning, but when the service is over, I open it up for the youths for an hour. That's the only time they're allowed to play online games here. I picked Sunday because they have to respect the Sabbath and not play violent games or those that encourage illegal activities on Sundays in God's house." She grinned. "It's worked so far."

"You're here six days a week?"

"Yes. I feel this is important, so, as they say, I put my money where my mouth is."

She thought he was going to tell her she spent too much time at the center, and she was ready to give him a strong rebuttal. If Marielle read Russ right, all he did was

61

work. At least what she chose to spend her free time doing was to benefit others.

But after a few seconds of silence, he said, "I'll be back tomorrow then, at three o'clock."

He walked with her to the door, and after they exited, waited while she locked up. They made their way to the cars, and without saying anything else, he flicked the remote lock for his SUV, removed the bar and drove away rather fast, Marielle thought, for being in a parking lot.

As the taillights disappeared around the corner, Marielle couldn't help but wonder what had happened that Russ figured he didn't have any more miracles left.

The next afternoon Russ pulled into the parking lot right on schedule. Marielle's car, dented roof and all, was already there, along with another older model sedan that had seen better days. He applied and locked the bar on the steering wheel, slid out, hit the remote switch to arm the alarm system, then walked toward the building.

Church or not, he'd seen too many buildings like this when growing up — it was both old and run-down — and he didn't ever want to see another one, unless it was on a heritage Web site he was designing for a client.

This would have been his last choice, hands down, of any place he wanted to be. He'd almost told his boss that he really was going to take his doctor's advice, lie down and not leave the house for a couple of days.

But Russ had given his word that he would get the computers set up, and Grant had given his word as the corporate sponsor that the job would be completed. Russ was obligated. A man was only as good as his word, and he'd given it. Besides, he had yet another debt to pay, and God would have him make good on it.

So here he was, the third day in a row.

On the third day, He rose, according to the Scriptures.

The words echoed in his head. Russ had heard that statement over and over when he was growing up, when his mother had dragged him to church. He'd believed it then, and he still did. Except now, Russ could look at it more realistically.

He glanced up at the tarnished steeple. God was out there, all right, but God had only made a difference in his life once, and he'd been paying for it ever since.

He knew all about trusting God and His miracles. Since then, Russ had grown a little older and a whole lot wiser.

Russ did all he could so he wouldn't ever have to pay again, and until his recent incident at the window, he'd had everything under control. For the past few years he'd been able to move forward with his life without owing anyone, including God. He'd worked, and he'd worked hard, and he was successful.

When he walked into the basement meeting room, he found Marielle sorting stacks of colored paper into piles, each accompanied by a ruler and a few miscellaneous pieces of white paper already cut into odd shapes. She made quite a comical picture, like she was getting ready for little kids, not a group of rough and rowdy teens.

He scanned the vacant computers, then looked back at Marielle. "What in the world are you doing?"

"I got a call from a friend who leads the Sunday school. The preschool level teacher was called away on a family emergency and they need someone to take over Sunday's class. I'm going to ask one of the girls to help me, but first we need to cut out a bunch of shapes so the kids can glue them together. They're too small to cut things accurately, and I'm not sure how good they are at gluing, but I don't know what else to do."

"You do this," Russ said, extending one arm to encompass the youth center room, "and you're going to teach the preschool on Sunday, too?"

"It needs to be done and there's no one else, so we have to make do. How are you feeling today?"

"A little better. I can't believe how long I slept. It must be the medication. I don't usually sleep over six hours, especially not on a weekday. Here comes Jason — I'd better get started."

But instead of joining him with the group at the computer, Jason sat with the girls who were cutting out colored shapes, guided by the white papers Marielle had already cut out, which Russ had figured out were templates.

Russ left what he was doing and joined the preschool table. The only chair available was in the center of a group of girls, so he stood behind Jason and rested one hand on Jason's shoulder. "How's it going, Jason?"

Jason turned and smiled up at him. "It would go better if you helped." He motioned with his head toward the one empty chair. "We've got to have lots of stuff ready for the little kids to make sure they're good and busy."

Russ stared in disbelief as the girls shuffled

out of the way, making room for him at the last empty chair, and worse, obligating him to join them.

One of the girls sighed as she slid one of the piles toward him. "I can't believe that I'm spending Friday night cutting out colored paper."

"It's for a good cause," Russ replied before anyone else could. If he had had someone to make him cut out paper circles on Friday nights, his youth would have been a lot different.

To his surprise, the rest of the boys filtered over to the table and began cutting out shapes, though they remained standing. When they finished, Russ figured they had the biggest pile of shapes, miscellaneous circles, squares, rectangles and triangles, he'd ever seen, and they'd finished in record time.

Marielle stood to address the group. "We did great. I think I'll order pizza for those of you who are allowed to stay."

In any other group, Russ would have expected all the teens to cheer, or at least show some enthusiasm, but in this group, showing appreciation was probably a sign of weakness. All they did was shrug, and no one said a word. At that age he'd had exactly the same bad attitude, until he saw that appreciating someone's extra effort was a way to get noticed by the right people, which ultimately helped him accomplish what he had to do. Still, he couldn't help but feel that these kids should have been more appreciative — after all, they were being rewarded.

"Do we get beer? It's Friday night," said a boy whose name Russ couldn't remember.

Marielle crossed her arms. "You know better than to ask that. First, you're underage, and second, this is a church."

The boy grinned. "I had to try."

"No, you didn't. Now clean up and I'll order. How many are staying?"

Not a single teen raised a hand, which of course Russ had expected. Marielle made a count just on slight nods or head shakes, then stopped and looked straight at him. "What about you, Russ? You helped cut the shapes, so you're invited to stay, too."

"Me?" He pressed one hand over his chest. "But . . ." He glanced around. The boys wouldn't look at him, but a couple of the girls did, and he could see by their imploring expressions that they wanted him to stay. "Yes, but only under the condition that you let me help pay."

Her relief couldn't have been more pronounced if she had a neon sign above her

67

head. "That would be great. Now if you'll excuse me, I'll be right back."

One of the girls approached him. "My brother once got his nose broken, except he couldn't go to the doctor. He's got a big bump now. Are you going to have a bump?"

Russ raised one hand to the bandage still covering his nose. "Probably, but the doctor told me it would be minimal." The bump he could handle. The doctor told him that while he was still out cold, they'd surgically straightened his nose, and because they'd done it right away, any permanent damage aside from the bump wouldn't be noticeable. He was just required to keep the bandage on for ten days to brace his nose until it healed sufficiently. While the bandage was ugly, he knew the bruise beneath it was worse — plus his nose was still quite tender.

If he had to say prayers, the one thing he was thankful for was the company's extensive medical insurance, something he hadn't had before he started working for Grant.

While the pizza was being ordered, Russ returned to the computers, but before he entered the next command, his cell phone rang.

He first checked the call display. "Hi, Grant," he answered. "What's up?"

"I didn't want to call you earlier in case you were sleeping, but were you at the office this morning, by any chance?"

Russ started keyboarding as he talked. "No. I actually spent the day in bed, just like the doctor ordered. Why?"

"When Brenda got here this morning, the door wasn't locked and the alarm wasn't set. Tyler said he was positive he locked up properly last night when he left. So we were wondering if you were in to get something this morning and forgot to lock the door."

Russ frowned. He would never, ever forget to lock the office door. Because of where and how he grew up, he was unfailingly diligent with anything where theft could occur. He even locked his car door when he went from his driveway into the house between bags of groceries after dark. "No. I wasn't there. Is anything missing?"

"No, nothing's missing, but it was just odd. The cleaning staff must have forgotten to lock up. I'm staying late, so I'll speak to the service tonight. There's too much valuable equipment in here for mistakes like that." He paused. "How's everything going down there?"

Russ glanced at the row of computers, only one of which was turned on. "It could be better. But I have a few more days, so

I'll get everything done just fine. I guess I'll see you Wednesday."

"Great. Bye."

Russ shut the phone and laid it on the table. He hit the prompt on the computer and waited for the next step of the installation.

Marielle sat in the chair beside him. "What's wrong? You look worried."

"The office was open this morning. Nothing was taken, but it's got me thinking. What kind of security does this building have?"

"There are good, strong dead-bolt locks on every door."

He turned around. "On the doors, yes, but I mean the windows. This is an old building. Have the original locks ever been replaced? Also, this is the basement, but there aren't bars on the ground-level windows and there should be."

"Bars? This is a church, not a prison."

"Thieves still break into churches. The bars wouldn't be to keep people in, but to keep unwanted guests out. Is there an alarm system for the building?"

"We can't afford an alarm. Besides, except for books and Sunday school supplies, there isn't really much to steal here. There aren't any expensive or ornate decorations, the sound system is all attached to the wall, and what isn't attached is old and well used. The treasurer takes the offering straight to the bank on Sunday mornings, so there's never any money on the premises. There's really nothing of value here."

"But now you've got five computers, and four more coming on Monday. I'm sure word has already spread through the community that they're here."

"Probably."

He rose, walked to the window and ran his hand along the bottom frame. "These are barely adequate. They should be enforced."

"This is a heritage building and we're on a low budget. Do you know how many windows there are in this building? I could ask a couple of the boys to go outside and see if they can figure out how to get in, to make sure the locks are secure."

"Are you kidding? That's just asking for trouble." He clenched his jaw and stared at her, unable to believe that she would invite kids who were already potential thieves a chance to prove themselves. "I've got another idea. I'll finish setting up the computers later. I have a little shopping to do, and I have to go quickly, before they close. Have you already phoned for the pizzas?"

"Yes."

"Call them back. While I'm out I'll pick them up, and that way we'll get a discount. See you soon."

CHAPTER FIVE

"What are you doing?" Marielle yelled over the sound of the drill.

"I'm making a hole," Russ said as he pushed down until he was all the way through the table. "This is much neater, to have the cables go through instead of stringing everything along the table and over back. But this is really to make sure everything stays put."

She watched as he tore open a package and, using the special glue, fastened a metal loop to the side of one of the monitors.

He turned to the teens who were watching every move he made, and said to Jason, "I'm still feeling a little banged up. Can you crawl under the table and stick this on the side of the tower?"

As he dotted the glue onto the flat section, Marielle stared at the hole in the table. "These are our banquet tables. When there's a special occasion, we use these upstairs. I was going to just put the computers on the floor when we need the table."

"Not anymore. This is now a dedicated computer table. I'm dedicating a second one on Monday, and they're not moving. I've already talked to Pastor Tom. I'm donating two new tables, so you won't be short. I don't feel good not having the computers secure."

He bent down to watch Jason attach the looped metal piece to the right spot. "Okay, Jason, unplug everything, will you?"

She stood back as Russ pulled all the cables up from the back of the table, then fed everything plus a plastic-covered chain back down through the hole. While lying on the floor, Jason plugged everything back in, fed the chain through the metal loop, now firmly attached to the case of the tower, then poked the end of the chain back up through the hole. Russ put the chain through the loop attached to the monitor and fastened both ends of the chain together with a small padlock.

"There. When they're all done, the only way these computers are going anywhere is to put everything below up onto the table, and carry everything out at once, and not through a window, but through a wide, double door. I can guarantee you that if a couple of thieves were to walk down the street carrying a banquet table with five computers strapped to it, they would attract attention." He paused and rested his hands on his hips. "Although, I wonder if it's possible to chain the table to the wall. . . ."

"This is good enough," Marielle said.

"Okay." Russ smiled, picked up the drill and revved it in the air. "One down, four more to go."

She expected to hear a Tim "The Toolman" Taylor grunt along with the noise of the drill, but it wasn't forthcoming.

Now that all the teens knew what they were doing, everyone wanted to help, but they only succeeded in getting in everyone else's way, especially since each had a piece of pizza in one hand and was eating while working. Russ showed considerable patience in letting them all do something, but it was slow going.

When the process was finished, a couple of the girls straightened and aligned everything on top of the table, and one boy swept up the wood shavings.

"Okay," Marielle called. "Enough time inside. Everybody out!"

Russ watched the teens file outside. "Out?"

"We play basketball every Friday night,

weather permitting. Some of these girls are pretty good, and they're all pretty tough when backed into a corner."

He frowned. "I don't doubt that. Tell me, what are you doing here, in this neighborhood? You don't seem like you belong here."

"A few years ago, there was a fire in my apartment building. Everyone got out okay and there was minimal damage to most of the suites, but they had to close the building for a few weeks for inspections, repairs, and then to get out the smell of the smoke. It was the middle of tourist season and there was a big convention in town, and by the time I started looking for a hotel, everything the insurance would pay for was full. A friend of one of my aunts lives not far from here, and she invited me to stay at her place for a few days, so I did, because I didn't have anywhere else to go. We made an instant connection. I went to church with her on Sundays, and the rest is history."

She didn't mention that Pastor Tom was the one who had given her the most emotional support and had guided her into doing something constructive with herself after Michael dumped her for another woman. Her own pastor had sided with Michael, telling Michael he had done the right thing, that they weren't really suited and it was just as well that he'd cancelled the wedding.

That was definitely true, but the way Michael had dumped her was cruel and heartless.

Her own pastor hadn't done anything to try to ease the hurt. In fact, it was Pastor Tom and a few people from this poor and needy congregation who had helped her deal with everything, including canceling many of the wedding arrangements. and it was then that Marielle had found the true meaning of friendship.

Besides, Michael and his new wife had started going to her other church, and she hadn't been comfortable there anymore. Now, two years later, she probably *could* go back and worship in the same room as them, but at the time, the hurt was too fresh. She just couldn't. Still, she would never leave this church and all the good people who helped her when she needed it. It was her turn to give something back, and she was.

"Didn't you have anyplace else you could go? Parents? Siblings? I've always been close to my mother and my sister, and I know if anything like that ever happened to me, that's the first place I would go."

"My parents travel a lot. It's hard to explain, but they really don't have a place to call home, at least not with a regular address. Not long after I got a job and got my own place, they came into a tidy sum of money. They sold their house, quit their jobs and got a motor home, and they've been traveling ever since. They generally stay someplace for a few months, and then move on. It's their goal to live for a while in every state, including Alaska, before they die. So far, they're doing pretty well." Marielle grinned from ear to ear. "You should see the pile of postcards I've collected over the past two years. And the pictures they e-mail to me are spectacular. My mother is talking about writing a travel book, and I think she should."

He blinked and stared at her, which was a common reaction when she told someone about her parents' adventuring ways. "Don't you miss each other? When do you see them? Do you have any other family?"

Marielle shrugged. "Of course I miss them, but we keep in touch. They're having the time of their lives, and I'm happy for them. They've planned to come visit me for Christmas this year, so that's going to be extra special. I'm an only child, and both my parents are also from one-child families, so it's just me here now that they're gone. But that's okay. I've got my church family here, and I'm happy. I haven't felt this right about a place, ever. God wanted me here, and so here I am."

She wanted to say that God had put her in the right place the day of his accident, too, but for the first time, he was asking her personal questions and she wanted to keep the conversation open. She didn't want to give him any reason to shut her out.

He turned back to the teens, who were dividing themselves in to two teams. "Do you ever play basketball with them, or do you just watch? Or do you referee?"

Marielle laughed. "I referee and try to keep the boys from getting too competitive."

"This I have to see."

"We've changed the rules to be less aggressive and more fair for co-ed. They abide by it, so it works for me."

They stood to the side to watch the scaled-down game until the sun began to set and the light became insufficient to see properly.

"Now what?" Russ asked, as all the teens moved back inside the building.

"I try to encourage them to play board games, but I'm not always successful. Usually we just sit and talk, and whenever I can, I try to steer the topic to an informal Bible study. They know this is a church, and they're bound to get stuck being forced to listen to some religious content as a condition of getting to use the facility. Some of them are believers, some of them are undecided, some of them aren't open yet, but they put up with me. I just do what I can, and I hope they make it through Saturday and come back on Sunday."

"Do they?"

"A few, but I wish it was more."

He mumbled something she couldn't make out, and chose to let it go.

This time, Marielle couldn't get the group to focus on anything but the new computers and the programs that Russ had brought and was going to teach Marielle to use, so she could in turn teach them. Again, she was reminded of the graphics program that most of them wanted to learn. It was the basis for a month-long course that a couple of their friends were taking at a significant cost.

When midnight came, Marielle saw all of them to the door, but instead of Russ following the teens out, he remained beside the table of computers.

"I couldn't do this with the kids watching. I can't keep the keys to the padlocks because at some point you might need to move them. I'm just not sure what to do. You're only here for a few hours a day. If some disaster happens and they need to be moved quickly, you shouldn't have the keys on you. I thought I should give them to your pastor, but he's not necessarily here all the time, either, and you're the one who spends the time in this room. If some emergency happens and they have to be moved quickly, both of you need access to the keys."

Marielle extended her hand toward him. "I'll just put them in the desk, then."

Russ shook his head. "No. That's too obvious. The point is to protect them from theft. The desk is the first place a thief will look for the keys." He glanced around the room. "This place is pretty bare." He looked up at the ceiling. "But . . ." His voice trailed off. "There's a place no one would look for keys. I could put them behind one of the ceiling tiles, and that way they'd always be close to the computers in case of emergency. I'll let Pastor Tom know where they are, and I think that would work the best. Both of you would have access, and if neither of you was here, you could just tell whoever was here where they were. All it would take is to stand on a chair, and you've got them."

That said, he pulled a chair to the end of the table. The effort to crawl onto the chair showed in his face, but he continued on his mission. Once he was standing on it, he was fine. He reached over his head, pushed up on one of the ceiling tiles, and slid the bundle of keys so they were situated directly above the computer that had formerly been his. When he let the tile drop, a cloud of dust poofed out, causing Russ to cough. He clutched his rib cage until the pain subsided and he could stand straight.

"Done," he said, then hopped off the chair.

The second he landed, he gasped for breath, his face paled, and again he wrapped both arms around his chest. "That was stupid," he said through clenched teeth.

Marielle also held her breath, unsure if he required medical assistance in case he'd dislocated something.

Slowly, he straightened and his color returned. "I'm fine. It's time to go."

She doubted he was fine. The only thing she could see that he was, was stubborn. "Will you be coming back tomorrow? None of the youth group will be here, and you promised that you'd show me how to run some of these programs."

"I did promise, didn't I?"

"If you're busy, that's okay. I'm sure we'll be able to figure them out from the help files."

"I'll be here. I promised, and the help files aren't the best way to learn these complicated programs. It might work better if I picked you up. If I go past your place to get here, it seems a waste of gas to have both of us driving."

Marielle's answer fled her brain. She could imagine the horrible gas mileage his SUV got, especially with the current gasoline prices. It didn't seem like someone who owned such a vehicle should be concerned with the price of gas. But now that she thought about it, he'd also saved her some money by picking up the pizzas and getting them the pickup discount. That he would be thrifty came as a surprise, but not an unpleasant one.

"Sure. I'll give you my address. I'll see you at two."

At one minute before two o'clock, an increasingly familiar, large SUV pulled into her driveway.

Marielle grabbed her purse, slid on her shoes and ran to the door. When she finished locking up, she turned around to see Russ standing on her porch.

"You could have waited for me in the car."

"My mother raised me to have good manners."

From what she'd seen so far, that was true, overwork ethics aside.

Just as he claimed his mother had taught him, he opened the car door, waited until she was settled in and closed it for her.

Not even Michael had done that. The last time anyone had opened and closed a car door for her was when she was too short to reach the handle and had to be strapped into a booster seat. She didn't know how to feel about Russ doing it. She didn't want to be impressed.

He glanced at her before turning into traffic. "Are you ready for this?"

Marielle nodded. "I brought a pen and a notebook to write things down, although I suspect I'll be reaching the point of brain overload in not too long."

"If that happens, we can just stop when you've had enough and pick it up again on Monday after I'm done getting the rest of the computers set up. I have to change the subject. Doing this learning session in the middle of Saturday afternoon, which is really your only day to do it, is going to take away the usable part of the day. When do you think you'll be able to get the repairs done on your car? Will it have to wait until next weekend? And I want to pay cash for the repairs so it doesn't affect my insurance rates."

"Yes. I'm not going to ask him to have a look at it on Sunday after church. That would be too much like asking a doctor for free medical advice away from the office. I don't mind leaving it. The door opens, the window still goes up and down, and it gets me to work on time, so anything else is extra."

His jaw tightened but he didn't reply, which told Marielle that she'd probably said the wrong thing. His SUV was in pristine condition, even though it was a few years old. Marielle's car, on the other hand, showed its age. She did care about her car and other personal property being in good condition and looking good — just not at the expense of what was really important, which was other people. Learning how to tutor the teens and being able to provide a few meals for the group was far more important than having a flat roof on her car. Besides, the dent wasn't bad unless she really looked at it — which she never did.

She turned toward him and watched him in profile as he drove. "While we're talking about that, I was wondering if anything has come back yet, if you've been able to remember anything."

"No, but since we're on the subject, I was thinking you might be able to tell me something that might jog a few memory cells. Can you tell me what you saw, and if you heard anything beforehand? Anything odd or out of place that would indicate what happened?"

"I didn't see or hear a thing. I had just picked up my ringing cell phone, which was why I pulled into the driveway and out of traffic. But there is something I thought was odd, now that you mention it. After you slid off the roof and landed on the hood, I ran out to keep you from falling onto the ground. I remember looking up, and now that I know exactly where your office is, I saw a woman's head stick out of your office window. That should have been normal, considering what happened, but I thought then that it seemed a long time before someone actually came out of the building to see what happened. Then, after the policeman had asked all his questions, the people you work with were outside, gathered together, standing around in shock after the ambulance left. But the woman who stuck her head out the window wasn't there. I thought if she was the first one to see that you'd fallen out, she should have been the first one down. She wasn't. She didn't even come outside. Unless she went outside after I left."

"There are only a few women who work in the office — it's mostly men. Can you describe her?"

"I was looking up into the bright sky, so I didn't see her very clearly, and she was up on the third floor. All I could tell was that she had dark hair and was wearing a yellow top."

"Was she wearing glasses?"

"No."

"Then it was either Brenda or Jessie."

"I wish I could tell you more."

"Well, thanks anyway." The church came into view. "Here we are. Are you ready?"

"As ready as I'll ever be."

Nothing more was said until they were sitting side by side at Russ's old computer, which appeared to be newer and had more memory than the rest of them. After he showed her the basics of the program everyone was anxious to learn, he gave her some assignments to do herself, which helped her understand the fine points. While she worked at the computer, instead of sitting beside her to watch, Russ picked up the drill and made four holes in the second table in preparation for the next batch of computers coming on Monday. As promised, they stopped when she felt she'd had enough.

On their way out the door, Marielle's stomach grumbled. Her cheeks heated up with embarrassment, but to Russ's credit, he didn't laugh.

"Want to grab a couple of burgers on the way back to your place?" he asked.

She assumed when he referred to more than one burger that he intended for them to eat together, which surprised her.

He also drove more quickly once they picked the burgers up, saying he didn't want them to get cold. She hadn't expected him to make the extra effort and was pleasantly surprised. The burgers were still warm by the time they were seated in her kitchen.

Before taking a bite, Marielle folded her hands and rested them on the table. "I always pause to pray before I eat. Will you join me?"

"Go ahead. I'll just listen."

Contrary to his claim, he did bow his head and close his eyes, which Marielle found comforting.

"Dear Lord, thank you for this food, and for the day Russ and I could spend together to learn. Amen."

"Amen," he responded.

Marielle bit back a smile. He had done

more than just listen, which she found both encouraging and curious.

She ignored her burger and fries, thunked her elbows on the table and rested her chin on her closed fists. "A couple of the girls have asked me what you look like without that bandage on your nose. I have to admit that the first time I saw you I had other things to think about, so I can't really remember what you look like without it. When does it come off?"

Russ's cheeks darkened, which Marielle thought quite endearing. He lowered his eyes and stared at his burger, also untouched.

"Friday. And I can tell you I'm counting the days. It may sound vain, but I want to know what I'm going to look like, too."

Brittany's comments about Russ probably being a "real hottie" echoed in her head. She tried to block it from her mind while she lowered her arms and began to eat. "When are you going back to work?"

Russ began to eat, as well, talking between bites. "Wednesday. That's why I put the holes in the tables today. I just have to get everything running, and I'll be done. If you still need some help learning the programs, I can come down after work."

"Thanks for the offer. I appreciate it."

"Jason seems like he has a good focus, more so than the other kids . . . er, I mean teens."

"Yes. He still needs to decide what he wants to do as a career, but he certainly loves computers. He types really fast, too."

"They don't call it typing anymore. They call it 'keyboarding.' "

"Right. And they don't call your speed 'words per minute' anymore. It's just 'keystrokes.' "

Russ told her a bit more about current computer trends and terminology, then stood. "I know you had plans that you cancelled. I think I'll go now so you call your friend back and see if you can still meet up."

She stared into his eyes, above the white bandage that still covered his nose. There was no hint of anything except honesty in them, and his question. Strangely even though at first she hadn't really wanted to spend the afternoon with him, she now was in no rush to go separate ways.

"Will I see you tomorrow morning?" The words were out of her mouth before she was thinking of what she was asking.

For an almost indiscernible second, he hesitated. "No. You won't. I'll see you Monday."

CHAPTER SIX

Russ found Marielle inside one of the closets Monday afternoon. "Marielle? What are you doing?"

She backed out, holding a couple of large bags. "I was just looking for more construction paper."

"I was going to ask you how the preschool class went at Sunday school. Why does it sound like you're doing it again next week?"

"Because I am. But at least this time I have more adequate notice. Do you need some help bringing in the rest of the computers?"

"They're still at the office. I called Grant, and he said he's going to be bringing them himself. He should be here any minute."

As if saying it made it so, Grant appeared in the doorway. "Russ? Marielle? Are you in here?"

"Here!" they called at the same time.

"Are you ready?" Grant asked, without

moving inside. "A few of the boys just got here and they're starting to unload my car."

Russ joined Grant at the door. "They can set them on that table, and they already know where to position them. Do you see what I've done to the other table?"

Grant nodded, telling Russ that he was impressed at how Russ had secured the first set of computers, and that the other table was ready for the second set. "Good work. I knew you were the right man for the job."

"Maybe so, but it's time for me to get back to my real job."

Grant turned to face Russ. "Unfortunately, there's been a complication."

"Complication?"

"Jessie still hasn't come in, she hasn't called, and her voice-mail box is full. Not only that, Byron told me that his funding has been put on hold for another project, and he requested that we put this on the back burner for at least a couple of months."

"That doesn't make sense. The last time I talked to him, he was pushing to have it done ahead of schedule."

"Whether it makes sense or not, that's the way it is. By the way, have you heard from Jessie? It isn't like her to behave this way. The only reason I know that she's not dead is that Tyler saw her downtown on the weekend. He said she waved at him as he was going up the escalator and she was going down, just like it was any normal day. He says he ran around and went back down, but by the time he got there, she was gone. Have you got any ideas? This all started the day of your accident."

Russ tried to think of a reason why Jessie might seem to be hiding, except at the same time, be in plain sight. "I haven't got a clue. I still can't remember what happened, much less why. But I have a question for you. Do you remember what Jessie or Brenda was wearing that day?"

Grant crossed his arms over his chest. "You're kidding me, right?"

"I wish I was. Marielle said she saw a woman with dark hair and a yellow shirt poke her head out my window after I fell. She also said that she saw everyone from the office outside after the ambulance left, and that woman wasn't in the crowd."

"Brenda was with me when the ambulance took you away. But now that you mention it, Jessie wasn't with the rest of us. When we all got back up to the office, she wasn't there, either. I just assumed she got so shaken up that she went home, and that she didn't tell anyone because we were all outside."

"So Jessie was in my office when I fell." Russ tried to remember what they might have talked about that day, but all he recalled was working on their client's project together, and getting frustrated with a glitch in his computer. He definitely couldn't remember what he was doing at the window.

The dizziness grew into a full-blown headache.

He pressed his fingers to his temples. "I can't remember what happened, but I just have a very strong feeling that this all has something to do with Jessie. And now that I know she was with me, at the very least she must have seen something. I really don't know how it's possible for me to just fall out the window. I go to that window and stick my head out for a breath of fresh air all the time." However, right now just the thought of sticking his head out the window brought on an almost dreamlike, terrifying sensation of falling, and with it, the headache pounded harder.

"Russ? Are you okay?"

"That headache is coming back again. I just need a couple of minutes and it will pass."

Grant's face tightened as he frowned. "I wasn't sure before, but I'm sure now. Between the recurring side effects of the concussion and because you still can't remember anything, I'm putting you on stress leave for a month. You work on all my most sensitive projects, so I need you to be at one hundred percent. You're not coming back to work until you've had time to relax and the headaches have stopped."

The headache increased to migraine proportions. "I can't be off for a month. I have so much to do!"

"No, you don't. You don't have anything important on your schedule because we'd cleared your calendar to allow you to work exclusively on Byron's project, and now it's cancelled."

"But . . ." He'd never been off work for more than a week's vacation. The concept of being off for a month was unthinkable.

He'd been working extra hard to get Byron's project done not one week, but two weeks ahead of schedule. He knew that Grant was looking to open up a new vice presidency, and Russ wanted the job. Completing one of the largest contracts in the history of the company ahead of a client's rush schedule would make him a shoo-in for the position.

Being on stress leave would not only stop him from completing the project, but take him out of the picture completely — the only time Grant would think of him was when Grant looked at his empty desk in his empty office. Russ knew that none of Grant's other employees could adequately fulfill his responsibilities or be dedicated enough to do all the extra work that was expected. Yet, if Russ wasn't there, he would be out of sight and out of mind. He feared that Grant might select the best of the staff available at the time for the promotion. If Russ wasn't there, it wouldn't be him.

"I think my time would be better spent helping everyone else with the current projects."

"I've been thinking about that all weekend, and especially all day today. I don't think that's true. You know I'm expanding the company, and right now, I need more exposure. The best advertising is word of mouth. If we can show the community, and then the city at large, how we put something back into the community, then we'll be on people's minds and they're more likely to think of us first. I know you're thinking that you won't know what to do with yourself if you're not at your desk working, but I have an idea. Instead of putting you on medical benefits, I'll keep you on full salary and I want you to spend your time here, at the youth center. It will bring us good PR."

Russ gulped. "Here?"

"Yes. Working here with the kids and teaching them how to use those programs will be a lot less stressful than being bombarded with everyone else's deadlines at the office. You need some time off, but I know you. You won't be content to rest at home. You need something to do, so I want you to work here. It will be a good move for both of us."

The headache stabbed through Russ's brain with such intensity that he thought he might vomit. He swallowed hard and sucked in a deep breath of air.

"It would be better if I was at the office. Why don't you send someone else here. Like Tyler?"

"Because Tyler doesn't need to take a break from the fast pace of meeting deadlines. Tyler needs to learn how to work with deadlines, and meet them. Like you do. I know I can always count on you to do what I need. And right now, I need some good PR, and this is an open door."

Russ forced himself to remain silent while a million thoughts ran through his head. He saw too much of his old life in Marielle's teens, and in this neighborhood. Years ago he had vowed he would never go back, that he would only move forward with his life.

And he *was* moving forward with his life. He'd found a good employer. Grant knew how hard Russ worked, and appreciated it. Grant also often gave Russ the hardest jobs because he knew Russ could handle them. And Russ did handle them.

But this was asking too much.

Still, Grant didn't know anything about where Russ had come from. According to Grant, he was just another guy from the suburbs. Grant judged him on what he was like now, not the insolent sewer-rat he'd once been. And what Russ was now was a loyal and dedicated employee.

He couldn't do anything to show Grant otherwise, because right now the key to getting the vice presidency was his willingness to put any program in motion that Grant desired, as long as it wasn't underhanded or illegal. Providing equipment and tutoring at an underprivileged teen center for a limited amount of time was far from either of those.

"Okay," Russ reluctantly agreed. "I'll do it.

Grant rubbed his hands together. "Great. I knew I could count on you."

"Yeah," Russ mumbled, hoping he looked more enthusiastic than he felt. He glanced at Marielle, who was openly staring at him, her eyes big and wide. He wondered if she was as surprised as he was that he was staying.

"It looks like they've got everything inside. I have to get back to the office. We'll be in touch," said Grant.

Russ watched in silence as Grant walked to his car and drove off. Then he turned to Marielle. "It looks like now we've got all the time we're going to need to sit down and show you how to use those programs properly. Since I'll be here, I can even help the teens myself for a while, if they need it."

"I'm sure they will. Most of them are pretty smart, but it takes a while to break down their defenses enough to get them to show it. It's more important for them to look cool and not act nerdy or geeky —" Suddenly, her face paled, then her cheeks flushed a brilliant red.

Russ gave her a half smile. "I'm not sure whether that's an insult or a compliment."

"To them, it's an insult, but please, take it as a compliment to you. I try so hard to convince them that after high school, those same geeky qualities are an asset and employers seek them."

"They do." Russ's computer skills and willingness to learn and advance had gotten him his job, and he hoped that what he was doing now would bring him more success in the form of a promotion. "So, that said, let's get started hooking up the rest of the computers. I've already noticed that six o'clock comes quickly."

Marielle fought the strange feeling that it was odd to be alone in the church basement. Five days a week, fifty-two weeks a year, she set up the room alone — going on two years now.

Today she felt differently, and she didn't want to think why the absence of a certain shiny silver SUV in the parking lot would mean anything to her.

Russ had told her that he'd already taken off the wrapping that supported his rib cage, but she wasn't interested in seeing him without a shirt. Okay, she was a *little* interested, but today was the tenth day after Russ's accident, so this day he had finally been allowed to remove the bandage from his nose.

Today was the day she was going to see what Russ really looked like.

She walked into the closet and began pulling out the boxes containing everything she needed to set up for their usual Friday-night activities. When the door opened and someone walked in, Marielle tried to hide her disappointment that it was only Jason.

Finally Russ entered, five minutes past his usual time. Marielle stared at him, too curious to turn away.

"Sorry I'm late. I —" He stopped, halfway between her and the door, staring back at her as she stared at him. He lifted his hand and touched the bridge of his nose.

Britt was right, Marielle thought, remembering the young girl's words. "How does it feel?" she asked.

"It feels much better without that stupid bandage. It was a little tender when the doctor poked at it, but if no one touches it, it feels fine. I'd hoped it wouldn't be the case, but there is a bump. The doctor said that sometimes it just happens. The important thing is that my nose is straight."

Marielle tipped her head just a little and studied him. She'd thought Russ was a handsome man even with the white bandage obscuring part of his face. He was, and she wondered why there wasn't a lineup of women following behind him. His eyes were unusual enough to attract attention, and she'd already thought the pale brown mixed with olive green and gold was a good match to his light brown hair. But now that she could see him as a complete picture, she was stunned.

His high cheekbones accented his rather

prominent nose, which she assumed had been perfectly straight before. There was a small bump at the bridge, but the surgeons had done a good job on the realignment. The bump would have looked natural if she hadn't known the nose had recently been broken.

But Britt was right. She imagined perfectly what he would look like, the day she called him a "hottie." The little bump made him look slightly dangerous, even daring, which didn't fit with the Russ who sat behind the desk at his computer all day and every day, in his third-floor office downtown. So far she'd only seen him in casual business attire, khaki or dress pants, and always a button-down shirt.

She wondered what he would look like in snug jeans and a T-shirt, wearing dark sunglasses and a baseball cap, on backward.

Marielle shook her head. The image of Russ dressing like one of the boys in her youth group was absurd. Besides, she wasn't attracted to the bad-boy type. Then again, she was no longer attracted to the nose-to-the-grindstone corporate type, either.

The type of man she *should* be attracted to was somewhere in the middle. She just hadn't met him yet.

Russ started walking again, straight to his

old computer, which she thought rather amusing. Every day, he bypassed the original two old dinosaur computers, the four other computers Grant had brought the previous week, and the four other computers Grant had brought on Monday. Every day, Russ went straight for the same computer, the one that used to be his own.

The teens had noticed, too. It had come to the point where they all called it Russ's computer, even though it was donated and, technically, the church now owned it. Still, no one would touch it until after Russ had used it, and until he was off helping someone else.

He was definitely a man of patterns — or habits. Marielle still had to decide which.

As he did every day, he sat in the chair, planted his feet firmly on the floor and fit himself against the seat, his back perfectly straight, as she was sure he did at his office every day. He then raised his hands to the keyboard, positioning himself with good posture.

If he had said anything verbally to the teens about sitting properly and not slouching, Marielle knew what their reaction would have been. Yet, she'd already noticed that a number of them were following his lead.

He leaned to the side, pushed the button to turn on the computer, then sat back, back straight. Suddenly, he frowned and crossed his arms over his chest.

"This is odd," he grumbled. Instead of the usual pattern of data and the logo of the operating system, the screen remained black with white text across it. Russ leaned down, pushed the release button for the A drive and pulled out a disk. He hit one of the keys, and the computer resumed booting up.

"Look at this. Someone left a disk in here."

Marielle shrugged and walked to stand beside him. "If you'll give me the disk, I'll ask around and find out who it belongs to."

He held out the disk as requested, but then didn't let go when she grasped it. "You don't understand. Yesterday no one used this computer except me, because I was doing some updates. I never put this disk in. Unless you used it today and then turned it off, and left a disk in, that means someone else was using it between the time we left last night and when you opened up."

"That's impossible. No one is here during the day except Pastor Tom, and he has a computer in his office."

"If it wasn't you, then someone else was using this computer," he insisted.

He tugged the disk back. "I'm going to see what's on here." He slipped the disk back into the slot and opened the directory. "This disk is blank." He stared at the screen, then leaned back in the chair.

"Then no harm was done," said Marielle. "I think everyone is here. Let's get started."

When all the teens had moved into position, Russ gave them a demonstration on the next assignment, then sent everyone to a computer to try it themselves.

He turned to Marielle. "You're the one, above everyone else, who should be doing this. I wish we had one more computer."

"It's okay. I'm grateful for what we've got. The important thing is for the teens to learn, and they are learning, thanks to Grant's donation and your good teaching."

"But I won't be here forever. You have to learn this well enough to teach it when I'm not here, and you're spending less time at it than anyone else. Your sacrifice to let them have the computers first is noble, but not very practical."

"I don't know what else to do."

He ran his fingers through his hair. "Would you like to do the same as we did last weekend, and I'll go over it with you on Saturday? Only this time, we'll go out for a real dinner, not greasy hamburgers."

"I don't know." She knew he was right, and she wanted to take advantage of his offer. But with the bandage off, for the first time since they'd met, something seemed different. Spending the afternoon in the church basement upgrading her skills was one thing, but going out to dinner with a handsome man on a Saturday evening was too much like a date. At the same time, she felt she should go because she knew he wasn't exactly pleased about being forced to stay and work at the youth center instead of going back to his real job. She didn't need a degree in psychology or human behavior to see that. She couldn't help wanting him to be happy to be there, to enjoy himself, and to feel that he was there more than to simply fulfill an obligation. She wanted him to see that in doing good deeds for the teens, he was doing some good for himself.

But the main reason she was having a difficult time deciding about dinner was that he was too much like Michael. She'd fallen in love with Michael easily. He was dedicated, a hard worker, loyal, and just plain old easy to be with. But the things that had so strongly attracted her to him were the same things that drove them apart. Russ shared too many of those qualities, and she refused to fall into the same trap a second time.

But Russ's presence at the center was an opportunity she couldn't turn away, no matter how she felt about him personally.

"We both have to eat," he said.

"You make it sound so basic."

He looked at her like he couldn't understand what she meant. "I just remember that by the time we were finished last weekend we were both starving. This time let's plan to quit a little sooner, and we can eat something worthwhile."

"When you put it like that, sure. We can do that. Now if you'll excuse me, I have to finish putting my supplies together for the preschool class on Sunday morning."

"Have you got something prepared for later?"

Marielle nodded. "Yes. This time I made sandwiches. It's so much cheaper than pizza. I do that fairly often, and no one seems to mind."

"I didn't mean supper, I meant a Friday night activity. But since you mention it, do you feed this whole group every Friday night?"

"Most of the time. If they went home to eat supper, there'd be less chance they'd come back. Feeding them is a good way to keep them off the streets and not hanging out at the local convenience store waiting for trouble to happen."

"That's true," he said, nodding.

Marielle returned to the desk and again began cutting out shapes. She'd only cut out four when Russ joined her.

"No one seems to need my help, at least not yet. Can I do something for you?"

"I'll never turn down such offers. This time I need ovals like this, circles like this, and sections like this." She held up the different shapes for him to see. "We're making sheep, so that gives you an idea of the pieces I need."

"I remember making sheep. You're going to have them glue on cotton balls, right?"

"So you did go to Sunday school as a child. I thought so."

He lowered his head and began concentrating on cutting the perfect oval out of the black construction paper. "Yeah. I did the routine. Oops, I think I'm being called. Excuse me."

Before Marielle could comment, he was gone.

CHAPTER SEVEN

"Yeah. What a riot, huh?" Russ smiled at Marielle's laugh, which was warm, genuine, and simply made him feel good for being the one to make her happy. But his heart was pounding.

He was enjoying himself too much, proving that it had been far too long since he'd been out on a date.

Except this wasn't a date. This was work.

Sort of.

Marielle dabbed at the corners of her eyes with her napkin, something he'd never seen anyone do before. "That was funny. Does Grant know what happened?"

"Oh, yes, he knows. Tyler showed it to him before we fixed it. Except Grant didn't think it was quite as funny as everyone else." In fact, Grant hadn't thought it funny at all when one of their clients accidentally deleted a complicated flash sequence they'd spent days working on, and replaced it with an animated gif sequence his son had made that featured singing and dancing rodents. "We changed it as soon as we noticed, but of course Grant was moaning and groaning about how many people in the world would have seen it first."

Russ grinned at the thought. "Actually, almost everyone in the office had saved a copy of the animation on their own computers before we killed it off the client's Web site, it had been so funny." His grin widened. "I saved a copy, too."

Still smiling, she said, "I wanted to thank you again for all your help at the center. They're getting so much out of it."

"I'm glad to help." Not overjoyed, but he would settle for simply glad. He'd been helping at the center for nearly two weeks, and so far it wasn't as bad as he had thought it would be. But then, when the kids — and they *were* kids — were at the center, they weren't loose on the streets to cause trouble. He didn't know what they were like away from Marielle and her influence, but when Russ saw them, they were inside a church, being led by an adult church leader, and except for a bit of an overflow of bad attitude, they acted accordingly.

At that age, he hadn't been quite so well-behaved even though his mother had taken him to church and he'd done all the typical church activities. At the time, though, there hadn't been a youth group. There were only Sunday school classes, and in the summer, a low-budget vacation Bible school. When he was a child Russ had taken great comfort in God. He had talked to God, and God had listened. Then, as an adult, when he asked God for help, God did help. And Russ had been paying God back for his so-called grace ever since.

The waiter arrived with their meals, breaking Russ out of his thoughts. He politely bowed his head and listened when Marielle prayed quietly over their meals, and his answering "Amen" slipped out without his thinking about it.

He didn't want to get dragged back into the church life, but he found that when he was with Marielle, thinking about God, and thanking Him, almost came naturally. Russ didn't want to think that Marielle could influence him in his decision to step back from God and everything God wanted, but then again, he wasn't so sure that what he was doing was necessarily a bad thing, either.

As she took her first taste of her chicken, Marielle closed her eyes and sighed. "This is so good! Thank you for bringing me here."

Russ glanced around the restaurant. It was nothing special or fancy. It was just a cozy little family restaurant with red-and-white-checkered tablecloths. It specialized in home-cooked meals instead of burgers and fries.

"Will you quit thanking me for everything? I told you, we have to eat, and with a little planning we can eat well."

She smiled graciously, causing Russ's stomach to do a little flip-flop, although he didn't know why. All he could do was watch her as she ate. Her hair was combed but not curled, and that gave her red streak more prominence. She wore jeans and a casual sweater, making her look more relaxed than she usually did.

"Okay," she said. "It's just that I don't usually go to places like this, and I just —" The musical ring tone of Marielle's cell phone cut off her words. She fumbled in her purse, checked the call display and flicked it open. "Hi, Brittany. What's up?" Her eyes widened and her mouth dropped open. "No! That's awful! No, don't worry about church tomorrow, and you can tell Erin not to worry about it, either. I'll see you next week. Bye."

She turned to Russ, all earlier traces of joy gone. "I just lost my two helpers for tomorrow morning. Brittany's mother had an accident where she works. Since it happened on the job, her medical is covered, but Brittany has to stay home and look after her brothers and sisters. Erin is going to go help her. That means I'll be all alone to look after twenty preschoolers. What am I going to do?" she moaned.

"Aren't any of the other kids, er, *youths* going to be there?"

"I heard Jason say that he was bringing Colin for the first time, so I can't ask them to do preschool."

Russ spoke quickly before he changed his mind. "Then I can help you. How hard could it be? They're just kids."

Her brows quirked. "Are you serious? Do you know what you're saying?"

"I know I'm not a parent, but I was a kid once, too."

"And you think that qualifies you?"

"I don't know. What qualifies Brittany and Erin?"

"Uh . . . that they're girls?"

"Is this discrimination?"

"I didn't mean it that way. It's just that girls are better, uh . . ."

"Girls are better mothers? That's true, but men are better fathers."

"Are you really sure you want to do this?"

Russ stopped to think. Did he? The reason he had offered was that she needed the help. But at the same time, he'd been thinking all week long that it was unfair that he was collecting a full salary from Grant, yet only working at the youth center Mondays through Thursdays three hours per day — nine hours on Fridays.

This week, he could count the four hours he'd spent today, but this was an exception — not that he would mind spending a measly four hours at the center on future Saturdays. Still, even if he did volunteer, although it wasn't exactly volunteering when his boss ordered him to be there, he would have to work thirty hours on Sunday to even come close to hitting the number of hours he usually worked in a week.

"What kind of time frame are we looking at for Sunday?"

"I have to be there early to set up, and then I bring a lunch for any of the youths who want to stay. We eat, and then Sunday is the one free day for playing online computer games. We usually finish up midafternoon."

Russ mentally counted. "So including lunch, that means another six hours."

"Something like that. But I certainly don't expect you to stay for all that time. That would be asking too much."

Thirty-one out of sixty hours.

"It's not too much. Trust me."

Marielle beamed, and Russ tried to tamp down his elation.

"That's great." She told him the basics of controlling preschoolers, and then the basics of handling the parents, which was apparently another challenge.

Russ found her instructions rather amusing, but tried to take them seriously because she had to be telling him for a reason.

When the waiter came to collect their plates, signaling the end of their cozy dinner, a pang in Russ's chest told him that he was sorry it was over.

He was jolted when Marielle reached for the bill. Russ covered her hand with his, halting her movement.

She looked up at him.

And his breath caught. Marielle had beautiful eyes. Most days he couldn't decide if they were green or grey because they changed depending on what she wore, or what mood she was in. Today, they were a darker green, and bright — almost dazzling in their greenness. He'd never seen such vivid eyes. He'd also never had the opportunity to gaze into her eyes so openly. They'd often been closer together, crowded side by side as he taught her things on the computer, but even though they were almost touching, they always had their attention on the computer.

Right now, the only thing he was focusing on were Marielle's gorgeous green eyes.

Her hand shifted beneath his. He feared she was going to pull away, so he automatically wrapped his fingers around her hand, holding it, feeling the warmth and enjoying the contact, even in its limited capacity, using the guise of not allowing her to scoop the bill out of the small tray as an unspoken excuse for holding tighter.

"No," he said, his voice coming out rough and gravelly, not at all like it should have.

"What are you doing?" she asked. "You said it was okay that I was paying for my own."

Russ cleared his throat, hoping words would come out normal this time. "I changed my mind. I was the one who chose to come here instead of someplace cheaper, so that makes it my responsibility to pay. You can pay next time we go out."

"Next time?"

"I'm sure we'll need to do more one-on-one tutoring just you and me next Saturday, too. Jason was right — there are entire month-long courses dedicated to learning that program properly. You need more time to learn it than just two easy lessons. Not to mention the other programs . . . "

"The lessons aren't really so easy."

He gave her hand a gentle squeeze. "No. They're not. But you're doing really well." Keeping her hand enclosed in his, he pulled the bill out from beneath their joined hands with his free one, left it on the edge of the table and pulled out his wallet.

"What are you doing?" she asked, looking down at his hand holding hers.

"Keeping you hostage. I don't trust you. I haven't known you for that long, but it's long enough to see that you can be stubborn when you want to be."

He also knew that all the meals she provided to the youth group had to be a financial sacrifice for her, which made him want to help ease the burden in the only way he could.

"I'm not stubborn. It's called determined."

"Right. I'm determined, too. I'm also bigger than you, so I win by default."

"You're being unfair."

"Sometimes life isn't fair, and this is one of those times. This is my treat, and that's that."

She sighed, signifying that he'd won, even

though it hadn't been a battle. It had been a challenge, though, and he liked that.

He had to let her hand go when the waiter appeared to take his credit card.

He was fine chatting in his SUV while he drove her home, but by the time he walked her to her front door, he'd begun to wonder if perhaps Grant was right — that blow to his head and subsequent concussion had affected him more than he thought.

What he was doing and the way he was thinking about Marielle was wrong.

He didn't have time to think of Marielle, or any woman. He was too busy to date when he had his career to consider — especially now, when he was right on the brink of getting the promotion that would be the crowning glory of all he'd worked for to this point.

Marielle was being nice to him because she had a goal, too, and that was to do the best for the teens who came to the center. He was a means to that goal, and Russ knew it. He could accept that, and he'd gone into the arrangement knowing that.

But that didn't stop him from having a gut-deep urge to kiss her good-night. He was human, and he was male, and he was seeing a pretty woman to the door after taking her out for dinner. He'd thoroughly enjoyed himself, and he was pretty sure she had, too. In any other circumstance, the night would have been a date.

But it wasn't a date. It was work. For both of them. For him, it was paid work; for her, it was volunteer work. But it was still work.

He felt no regret — that was the way it was. She'd once called herself practical. He was practical, too.

The second the door opened, Russ backed up a step, just to avoid temptation.

"I'll see you in the morning," he said. "I know you're nervous about it just being the two of us, but it's okay. They're just little kids. Everything will be fine."

"How did it go?" Jason asked as he walked into the now-deserted classroom.

Russ stared blankly at the wall. "Good. I think. I'm not sure. Marielle? How did it go?"

She turned to Jason, and Colin who was standing behind Jason. "It went well. Russ was a great helper."

Russ turned and stared at the kiddie-sized tables, which were so low they barely came up to his knees. And thinking of his knees, they ached from so much squatting. From this day forward, he knew he would have a greater respect for athletes and the deep knee-bend exercises they were required to do. Athletes, and preschool teachers.

The tables were littered with so much cut paper that he could see only a few places where more than a couple of square inches of the table's surface showed through. Cotton balls were spread everywhere, more on the floor than the table. And the glitter. Marielle had warned him two seconds too late not to let the children hold the container. He was positive that glitter had been condensed and vacuum packed, because that was the only way he could account for the volume now coating the floor.

"Jason, would you mind getting the broom out of the closet in the hall?" Marielle asked. "Here's the key."

"Did anyone get the license number of that truck?" Russ asked. "What hit me?"

"About seventeen four-year-olds. But you lived, and I think it's time to celebrate. As soon as we clean up, we can eat. I brought lunch."

He slowly took in the disaster in the room. It had been difficult enough to keep the children busy and entertained and ignore the ever-accumulating mess. Then came the mayhem of trying to control the children and make sure none of them snuck out of the room unnoticed before their parents arrived to pick them up. The whole morning had made his brain go numb. The worst day at the office was nothing like this.

Yesterday Russ would have argued and insisted on going to a local pancake restaurant for a warm meal. Today, cold sandwiches made the night before and warm-enough coffee out of a thermos sounded like a taste of heaven.

"I could go for lunch. Where is it?"

"Under the desk. But first you have to finish cleaning up all that glitter. Here comes Jason with the broom."

"I might have underestimated the magnitude of this project."

To Marielle's credit, she bowed her head to hide her smile, but he still saw it.

"Do you have to do this again next week?" he said, staring at the devastation.

"The regular teacher will be back, so everything will go back to normal."

"That's a relief." He accepted the broom.

Jason picked through scraps of paper on the table, saving the bigger pieces and putting them in a box, and throwing the smaller pieces into the recycle bin, while Colin walked around the room picking up all the cotton balls.

"Doing this makes me appreciate my regular group by tenfold, as the Bible says,"

Marielle said as she walked around the room gathering the glue and scissors.

He could certainly understand that.

Russ set to work carefully sweeping up the glitter, and with all four of them working, they were done much more quickly than he'd anticipated.

"Great," Marielle said. "Now let's go to the youth center room and we can have lunch." Marielle reached for the coffee thermos, Russ reached for the small cooler, and the boys ran ahead.

Russ walked side by side with Marielle down the empty hallway. He couldn't believe how fast the building had cleared out, but then it was lunchtime, and *he* remembered being anxious to leave the church back in the days of his youth when he'd attended regularly. The only sound beyond their footsteps on the tile floor was the jingle of Marielle's keys as she pulled them out of her purse.

Russ felt comforted to note that the room had been properly secured, even from the inside of the building, when the Sunday school finished with it. Jason and Colin stood aside while Marielle unlocked the door. As was becoming a habit, Russ went straight for his old computer.

"Russ? What are you doing?"

He grinned. "Today is Game Day. I've been known to play an online game or two. Am I allowed?"

She mumbled something about stupid computer games under her breath that he chose to ignore.

"Hey," he said as he sat down. "My computer is on."

Marielle's brows crinkled as she joined him. "That's odd. Everyone was told not to touch the computers, and they haven't before. I'll talk to the Sunday school superintendent to remind the teachers that the kids aren't supposed to be allowed near the computers. Unless we forgot to turn it off when we left on Saturday."

Russ never forgot to power down his computer. Ever.

He rested his hand on the monitor. "It's only slightly warm, meaning it hasn't been on for that long."

"That's really strange. I thought everyone else besides us left at least half an hour ago."

"Then the screen saver should have been on. That means that whoever was using it left less than seven minutes ago."

"I guess we just missed them, then. Let's eat. I think everyone is hungry."

Russ was hungry, too, but he lingered at the computer while Marielle walked to the rear door that led directly outside and opened it.

They had been making a fair amount of noise while cleaning up and talking among themselves, but he had the impression that the whole church had been deserted for a while. Even the pastor had locked up and was gone. It seemed odd that someone had been in the building. Both doors to the youth center room had been properly locked. The outer door had a proper dead bolt, but the door leading to the hallway for the rest of the church was a simple indoor lock that could be engaged without a key.

While Marielle removed the sandwiches from her cooler, Russ checked the other computers, first the eight that Grant had donated, and then the two that were the church's originals. All were cold, as they should have been.

He rested his fists on his hips and stared across the room at his old computer. They never had found out who left the disk in the drive, and he suspected the same would hold true of whoever left the computer on today.

One thing was confirmed, though. It was good that he'd chained all the computers together securely through the table. Just because this was a church didn't mean that property was exempt from thievery. Even if it was purely innocent, which it probably was, he still didn't like unauthorized people using the computers without permission.

"Come on, Russ."

"Sorry. I'll be right there," he said as he went to join her.

As before, Russ bowed his head while Marielle prayed and answered her "Amen." Strangely, he couldn't recall ever being so thankful for a simple sandwich. He sat with Marielle at the desk to eat, while the two boys ate beside the computer, something he would never have allowed if he had been in charge.

"Are you expecting any more today? It seems kind of stark, with only two boys in here."

"A few more will probably come in about half an hour. The number varies. When the weather is nice, fewer come."

True to Marielle's prediction, four more boys arrived, but no girls.

"I guess the restrictions on the games are okay if they still come. Do you ever play the games with them?"

"Yes, sometimes, but not today." She glanced quickly from side to side. "Now that the games have begun and we're alone, I have something here for just the two of us. I thought we'd need it after a morning with the preschoolers."

Russ stared as Marielle pulled a couple of specialty chocolate doughnuts out of her cooler. "I hope you like these. They're my favorite, and I think this is a good time for a good old-fashioned chocolate fix."

"Thank you. I don't know what to say."

"I wanted to do something to show you how much I appreciate your help. I couldn't have done it alone."

"Mmm. This is good," he said as he nibbled the sweet doughnut. But more than he enjoyed the rich chocolate and thick crème filling, Russ appreciated Marielle's generosity. He knew that she treated her entire group to dinner on Friday nights between the regular after-school meeting and the Friday night don't-get-into-trouble activity sessions. She also appeared to bring lunch every Sunday for anyone who wished to stay. He was impressed with her giving spirit, whether he wanted to be or not.

"This is a real treat, to have six of them all involved in the same game on different computers. We've never been able to do this before. In the past we allocated each blocks of time based on how many came, in order to be fair. This will do a lot to bring them here during the week, when we are in a learning curve."

Part of him thought that was good, and he was glad to help, but a deeper part of him wanted to run and hide from the unpleasant memories that being with such a group evoked. Until the accident, he had been comfortable in his routine, and now it was disrupted.

When their time was up, Russ double-checked all the computers to make sure they were off, and waited while Marielle locked up.

During the drive home, he and Marielle laughed at some of the bizarre things the children had done during class time. The trip ended too quickly, and he found himself walking Marielle to her front door, even though it was the middle of the day, just to make the time with her last longer.

"I guess I'll see you tomorrow, then," he said while she inserted her key in the lock.

"Yes. I've got you for three more weeks, and I plan to take full advantage of you. I heard what the boys were saying about you — you're making quite an impression."

"I'm just doing my job." He backed up when the door opened. "Goodbye." He turned and headed back to his SUV.

As Russ drove home all he could think of was that he *didn't* want to make an impression. He only wanted to teach them what they needed to know, and to supervise and help them understand computers better. And then his commitment was over.

Three more weeks.

In so many of the things the youths did, he saw echoes of the way he used to be, and the reminder was something he wanted to leave in the past, where it belonged. Three more weeks was too long, but yet at the end of those three weeks, he would have no more reason to see Marielle. The feeling that thought evoked sat badly in the pit of his stomach.

He walked into his house, his stomach still upset. About this same time yesterday, he'd been walking into the restaurant with Marielle, about to spend a very enjoyable evening with her.

But today, it wasn't to be. They'd had their time together. Marielle had made sandwiches for a quick and easy lunch. Today, for supper, he was sitting in a cage of his own making, and he was eating alone.

First he took his package of antacids out of cupboard, and then he began making dinner for one.

CHAPTER EIGHT

Marielle nearly jumped out of her chair as the youth center room's door banged open. A large crowd of boys filed in, laughing and talking loudly, followed by a second, even larger group. Right behind the second group came a throng of girls, only they were more quiet.

Marielle noted they were earlier than usual, as well.

She pushed away the surge of jealousy that they were coming for Russ, telling herself this was what she wanted to do, to give the teens a place they wanted to be, versus someplace convenient to hang out when there was no place else to go. That they were coming with more enthusiasm and in greater numbers because of Russ meant nothing. The point was that they were coming.

She'd also noticed that instead of gathering in the corners of the room, the girls were congregating at the end of the table opposite Russ. Marielle gritted her teeth. How the girls felt about him was of no concern to her. He was a mentor and a teacher, and in three weeks, he would be gone.

Three weeks.

Though he was only a temporary apparition, the place would be different without him.

This time, without the distraction of needing to prepare for the Sunday school, Marielle was able to give her full attention to Russ as everyone surrounded him at the computer. When the demonstration was completed and all the teens sat at different computers, he did as he did every day — he walked around checking periodically on everyone, and then spent time talking to Marielle.

This time her hands were free.

"You should be sitting at one of the computers and trying to enhance one of the graphics, like everyone else."

"I don't mind. This program is for the kids' benefit, not for me."

"Ah, you called them 'kids,' " he said, lowering her voice to almost a whisper.

She smiled. "They can't hear me. And I know you won't tell."

"You might have to bribe me. Got any

more of those doughnuts?"

Marielle rolled her eyes. "I think Sal is having a little trouble over there."

All traces of Russ's gaiety dropped. "You're right. I should have been paying more attention. Excuse me."

Marielle watched him go.

Excuse me, he'd said.

He was always so polite, and so . . . just plain nice.

She didn't want to like him. Michael had been easy to like, too. And it had nearly been the death of her. She'd given up too much for Michael, including her college education.

She'd felt so worthless when Michael dumped her. Now, at nearly thirty years old, all she had was an office job, no savings and no education. She'd lost the best years of her life, and she would never get them back. Yet, between her job and her volunteer work she felt that she had her life in order — she was happy. She was comfortable just to be herself, she didn't have to care that she wasn't meeting someone's higher standards or expectations. She also was allowed to make mistakes, although she hoped that didn't happen too often.

That was one of the main differences between Michael and Russ. Russ seemed very down-to-earth — a real person. He even had a sense of humor, which a man who worked with a room full of preschoolers armed with glitter and glue sticks definitely needed.

Except he worked obsessively, just like Michael. She was sure Russ hadn't seen that she'd noticed, but a few times she'd watched him press one hand into his stomach in a tense moment, telling her that if he didn't already have an ulcer, he was on the verge of developing one.

When everyone finished their current project, one by one they shut their computers off and went home for supper, until just Marielle and Russ remained.

Surveying the empty room, she said, "I guess this is it for today. Again, thanks for all your help, Russ."

"That's what I'm here for." He pressed one hand over his stomach. "It's suppertime. Would you like to join me?"

She wanted to. She really did. But at the same time, it wasn't a good idea.

"I'm sorry. Not this time." She almost continued on to suggest that maybe another time would be better, but that would have been wrong. Another time *wouldn't* be better because she knew what it could lead to. She liked Russ too much . . . and she wouldn't go down that road again.

An odd expression crossed his features. "Okay. I'll see you tomorrow, then, for more of the same."

More of the same.

Marielle didn't know if that was good or bad.

Russ refused to let being home with nothing to do day after day get to him.

His house was the cleanest it had ever been. His lawn was so neatly trimmed and the shrubs so shaped to perfection that the neighbors were talking about them. His fence had two brand-new coats of paint. His SUV shone so brightly that it reflected the colors of the rainbow.

Russ was so bored he thought he could scream.

That would really get the neighbors talking.

At precisely two-thirty, Russ checked his hair and left. He arrived at the center fifteen minutes early, just like the day before. And just like the day before, he walked into the church through the main door and headed for Pastor Tom's office.

"Hey, Russ. It's good to see you again."

"Hey, Tom. It's good to see you, too." Russ meant it.

Tom looked up at the clock. "I've been meaning to ask you, how's it going with the youth center? I know sometimes those kids can be a challenge."

"Don't call them kids. They're not adults, but they're certainly past childhood. They're teenagers." The second the words came out of his mouth, echoes of Marielle telling him the same thing floated through his consciousness.

Pastor Tom's mouth curved upward good-naturedly. Little crinkles appeared at the corners of his eyes. For the first time, Russ noticed a touch of gray at Tom's temples. That added a bit of wisdom to Tom's friendly appearance. "Sorry. You're right. Are you doing okay with them?"

"They're actually a good group, at least while they're here. Marielle has very specific codes of conduct outlined. They follow them or they aren't allowed back."

"Those computers your boss donated have made a big difference. I'm not going to belittle Marielle's work and dedication, though. No one has been able to get a handle on that group like she has. I don't know how she did it, but they're very loyal to her."

Russ thought of the way the group responded to her. The girls definitely looked up to her, and she would be safe in a dark alley with any of the boys nearby.

Russ grinned. "Maybe it's that red stripe in her hair. When we first met, that's the first thing I noticed."

"I remember when they did that. It was on a Friday night, and everyone who stayed into the evening did something wild with their hair. Even the boys put in colored streaks. It just grew out faster. I couldn't believe she used permanent color."

That was Marielle. She never did anything halfway. It was always all or nothing. He actually liked the stripe in her hair, and he thought it suited her. It was bold and dynamic and by no means subtle, just like Marielle. When she wanted something, she went for it and nothing would stop her, no holds barred.

"By the way, Russ, while we're talking about Marielle, do you mind if I ask you something?"

As far as Russ could tell, Tom seemed to be doing all the talking about Marielle. "Go ahead."

Pastor Tom leaned back in his chair and crossed his arms over his chest. "How's she doing?"

"I'm not sure I understand the question."

"I don't know if she ever takes a break.

She has a full-time job, then she comes here and looks after the youth center until suppertime. Most people would think she has the evenings to relax and do whatever she wants, but it doesn't quite work that way. For the past two weeks she's looked after some of the Sunday school, as well, and once a week she's a volunteer counselor here in the main office. She's been going solid with no break for seven days a week lately."

A surge of guilt hit Russ as he mentally counted her time on his fingers. Pastor Tom was indeed correct. Marielle started her regular job at six in the morning in order to be at the youth center so early after work. Counting backward, he thought she had to get out of bed before five in the morning to be on time. He worked long hours, too, but not as long as Marielle's combined hours. He at least had time in the evenings to wind down and do what he needed to do before the next day began.

"You're right. Now that you mention it, to get eight hours' sleep she'd have to be in bed before nine, and I don't think she does that. But I haven't noticed her being overtired or stressed out." In fact, he'd been far more stressed than she had when trying to deal with the herd of hyperactive preschoolers. She'd taken everything in stride, and even laughed about it, while he'd thought he'd been run over by a truck.

"Good. I just want to make sure she's okay. Sometimes I worry about her working too hard, that she's overdoing things."

"If I understand what you're asking me, I can make sure she takes some time for herself to wind down. I'm off work for a couple more weeks, so I'm in a forced relaxation mode, and I need something to do. Helping Marielle so she doesn't do everything herself sounds like a good idea." Focusing on something besides his four walls would go a long way to helping him keep his own sanity, as well.

"Great. Now let's get that room open for you."

The halls were empty as they walked toward the youth center room. "By the way," Russ asked, "does anyone else have a key for that room?"

"Yes. Every one of our church elders has keys for all the rooms. Why do you ask?"

Russ had been hoping for an easy solution, but it was not to be. "It's just that someone was using one of the computers and left it on."

"I'll mention it at the next board meeting."

The pastor opened the inside door of the youth center room at the same time that the outside door opened.

"Hey, Marielle."

She jumped at the sound of his voice, which caused her to nearly drop a bag she was carrying. Her purse slipped out from under her arm, and she fumbled with the bag to prevent her purse from falling to the floor. Once she recovered the bag and the purse, she stood, clutching both to her chest, and around her legs, her flowing skirt swished in the breeze from the open door. She looked so disheveled, he wanted to help her even though she now had everything under control. She stood staring wide-eyed at them from across the room.

"Don't do that! You guys startled me."

"You're earlier than usual." Russ gulped, trying to push the thought that he had actually wanted her to ask for his help out of his mind.

"Traffic was really good," she said as she removed a stack of disks from her purse, then locked her purse in the desk drawer.

"I'll be going now," said Pastor Tom from behind Russ. "It's not a good idea for this group to see the pastor in here. Too much religious influence. I'll probably see you tomorrow."

Russ nodded at Pastor Tom as he left, then turned to Marielle just as she knocked over the pile of disks. In a few strides, he was at her side, helping her restack them. "That's quite a pile you've got there. Why are you here so early?" Not that fifteen minutes was that early, but he knew where she was coming from and what time she got off work.

"My boss let me leave early. I have a feeling she's got a project in mind for some of the youth group, and of course we don't charge, so she saves paying the overtime for what it would cost someone else to do it. We do each other favors that way. But this is something different. I got an idea last night after I got home. I brought some clip art and images for everyone to start on a brochure for the church's Valentine's Day banquet."

"But that's months away."

"Then we'll have lots of time."

He frowned. "I hate to start a project then walk away in the middle of it."

"That can't be helped. I wanted to start this now, while there's professional help available."

The words were out of his mouth before he had a chance to think about what he was offering. "Then I'll come back a few times when you're close to done, in case anyone needs extra help."

"Really?" she asked. Russ tried not to feel stung by the obvious surprise showing in her expression. "That's so nice of you. That would be wonderful!"

"Yeah, well —"

A male voice cut off Russ's reply. "Hey! Russ! Marielle!"

Russ turned around to see Jason and Colin walking through the door. "Does no one ever say 'hello' anymore? Since when did 'hey' become a salutation?"

"You do it all the time." Marielle paused while one corner of her mouth tipped up. "I've heard you. You did it just today."

Russ thought back to his earlier greeting, and she was right. The group was rubbing off on him, telling him what he feared was coming true. He had begun the downward spiral. It was so subtle he hadn't noticed, but it had started.

He straightened his posture, and one hand rose to his neck, except here, he wasn't wearing a tie to fiddle with the knot. He dropped both hands to his sides, then rammed his hands into his pockets.

"It won't happen again," he grumbled, then spun on his heels and strode to his computer, turned it on and waited for it to boot up.

The group assembled quickly. He ran through as much as he thought they could retain in one session, then sent them to do the assignments he'd prepared.

This time, instead of talking to Marielle, he remained seated, except he found himself staring at the inactive screen because he was without a project to work on.

Marielle's voice drifted from over his shoulder. "Have you noticed that not only are all the computers filled today, there's at least two sharing at every station? We had a lot come last time, but today there are even more. I don't think I've ever seen this many. I've decided to make a change in the structure of what I'm doing. I brought doughnuts for everyone, and I need you to stop everyone in the middle of what they're doing so we can take a break and eat, and then I'll send them back."

"Why can't you wait until they're done?"

"Because I don't want them to leave. I'm going to say a quick prayer of thanks for the doughnuts, then send them back to the computers. If I wait until they're done, some of them might leave rather than join in when I'm praying."

He spun around in the chair. "That sounds a little calculated."

"Besides steering them away from gangs

and questionable activities, this is the real reason I want them to come here. So far we've only done informal talks and question-and-answer things, but it's time to kick it up a notch, as the saying goes. This is the only time some of them will ever get to open themselves up to God and the peace a person can have in their heart once they get to know Him. For some of these kids, all they see and hear at home is swearing and cursing and sometimes fighting. Drugs and alcohol abuse is out in the open — I know a few parents who don't even try to hide it. In other homes, even if everything else is fine, they face a life without a future because of the income level, and in this neighborhood they can't break out. All they get at home is discouragement and hopelessness. You don't know the atmosphere in some of the homes they come from."

"Yes, I do!" he snapped, unable to stop himself. "The one here who doesn't know what it's like is you. You talk about the hopelessness, but do you know what it's like to be so buried by disaster after disaster that you can't find a way out, so you just sink deeper and deeper? When you get so desperate and so angry that you'll do anything to get out?"

"Uh . . ." Marielle glanced from side to

side. Russ stared intently into her face as she looked him straight in the eye. Her voice dropped to barely above a whisper. "Do you want to talk about this? Like, uh, somewhere else?"

Russ swung around in his chair to face the computer. "No. I don't."

He began keyboarding, but as he did, he became aware that all noise in the room had stopped, all heads were turned and everyone was staring at him.

His hands stilled, poised over the keyboard, while a million thoughts rushed through his head. He didn't want anyone to think he thought he was better than them. He wasn't. He knew everyone was equal in God's eyes. God looked at the heart, not the bank account or how many bathrooms and bedrooms a person had in their house, or even if they didn't have a house at all.

He also didn't want to discourage anyone there from trusting in God and His power. He hadn't meant to challenge Marielle, and he certainly didn't want to challenge God. It was God who had set him free, yet at the same time, God hadn't loosed other chains that bound him.

He pushed the chair back and stood. "It's time for a break. Marielle brought doughnuts. They're on the desk."

In his mind, Russ pictured every one of the teens getting up and running to the doughnuts, jostling for the best ones.

No one moved. Because in this crowd, it wasn't cool to be the first to accept anything that might be construed as charity.

Russ's pride about accepting charity had long ago been squelched. He walked to the desk first, picked one of the best chocolate-covered crème doughnuts, and held it up for all to see. "You snooze, you lose," he said, then took a big bite.

Marielle smiled shakily and joined him. She selected a plain doughnut, and also took a bite.

"Sorry I wrecked your plan," he said softly so only Marielle could hear. "I know you wanted to pray first."

"It's okay. We'll pray next time."

A couple of the boys got up and sashayed to the desk, elbowing and hip-checking each other, to show that they really weren't in a rush and that free doughnuts weren't important.

Gradually everyone got up and helped themselves.

Russ ate his doughnut so slowly it was almost painful, just so he wouldn't be the first to finish, and to encourage the kids to relax after he'd lost it in front of them.

He would talk to Marielle later, in private as she'd suggested. He would apologize for his outburst.

Brittany shuffled in close to him, so close they were almost touching. "Russ, what did you mean about being desperate?"

He looked down at Brittany, so young but no doubt having been through a lot. He couldn't remember a time that he saw her when she didn't look tired. Even today, early in the week, circles rimmed her eyes, despite her attempts to cover them with makeup. He remembered that the reason he'd had to help Marielle with the preschool on Sunday morning was that Brittany's mother had an accident and Brittany had to care for her siblings. He hadn't thought about it at the time, but he now wondered where the father was. If Russ were a father and his daughter wanted to go to church, he would do what every father should do, and that was look after the other children so the one could go. Either the father didn't care enough to look after his own children, or there was no father.

He braced himself, knowing that whatever he said to Brittany would be heard by everyone. Russ was sure it would be repeated at the speed of sound, or maybe even the speed of light.

"Things haven't always been good or easy for me. There have been times I've struggled so hard I honestly thought it would never get better, and then when I thought it couldn't get worse, it did. But one day, it did get better, and it's stayed better, and I guess that's why I'm here."

They didn't ask what it took to get where he was now, so he didn't offer.

"You mean you weren't always rich?"

Russ nearly laughed, except Brittany was serious. "I'm not rich. I'm not even close. But I'm comfortable. I know this sounds callous, but you have to know that no matter how bad you think you've got it, someone else, somewhere, has it worse."

One of the boys whose name he couldn't remember took one step forward, still keeping his distance, but making it plain that he had something to say that he wanted the group to hear. "That's easy for you to say. You don't know what it's like to live in a neighborhood like this."

Russ considered the young man for a moment, then said, "Yes, I do. I come from a neighborhood just like this one. When I could, I moved to a different city where I could make a fresh start. And I can tell you a lot about having to accept charity, and accept it graciously. Money, used clothes, the foodbanks. You name it, I've been there. My mother used to tell me that it was okay to accept charity if one day, when you didn't need it anymore, you could give it back to someone else who needed it more than you. She used to quote me Bible verses that it's okay to accept things when done with the right heart, not like it's owed but out of gratitude."

Marielle turned to him. "Your mother sounds like a very special woman."

He felt the question she hadn't asked, which was whether his mother was alive.

"She is. She's remarried now, and doing fine."

Brittany stared up at him so intently he almost felt it. "What about your dad?"

"My dad left when I was about your age, and I haven't seen him or heard from him since."

"You got brothers and sisters?"

"I have a younger sister. When she was little she got hit by a car, a hit-and-run, and she was pretty bad for a while. They didn't know if Sasha was going to be permanently disabled. My dad couldn't take it, and he left."

A collective gasp echoed around him.

He glanced around the room; everyone was staring intently at him. "My sister is okay. One leg is a bit shorter than the other, and she limps and she wears special shoes, but she's otherwise okay. But it was hard on all of us in different ways. So don't tell me I don't know what it's like. I can tell you all this. I worked, I learned, and I worked some more. And if *I* could do it, *you* all can do it, too. In fact, if you swallow your pride, there are now agencies and programs that weren't around when I was your age. Take advantage of everything that's given to you, make something of yourself, and then when you're in a position to do so, give it back so someone else can get out, too."

Jason looked at him eye to eye, their heights matching. Jason was as big as a man, yet inside, in so many ways still a boy. "Is that why you're here? To give something back?"

Guilt swept over Russ. He wasn't here to give back. He was here for a purely selfish reason — to get ahead in his job. "No," he answered honestly, without expounding or making excuses. "Now let's get back to the computers. You're all doing well, but you've got a lot more to do if you're going to get as much out of this as your friends who took the course and had to pay money for it."

As he walked around to each of the teens, he thought every one of them was concentrating more and working harder than usual. Russ didn't think his speech had been motivational. He was sure that some of these kids had stories just as bad or worse than his own. Most people didn't know what really happened inside the walls of their neighbors' homes, or even their family's homes. Many people had known about his sister, but no one had known all the dirty details, especially after his father deserted them.

None of the teens looked at him as he talked to them — they kept their concentration fully on the computers. But Russ could almost feel Marielle's gaze burning into his back.

This time, when they were done with the assignments he'd prepared, instead of working on what Marielle had brought, they pulled the chairs into a circle and Marielle read them a few Bible verses on asking God for favors. Some of the people in the Bible, from the poorest poor to the richest kings, asked God for something, based on their need at the time.

Those who were willing to share discussed some of their needs, which Russ found a real eye-opener into the backgrounds of the kids he'd seen every day for the past two weeks. Just like he'd told them, he had no idea what their lives were like beyond the quirky smiles and displays of attitude.

Not one of them left before six o'clock. But when the designated hour came, they all departed at once.

Which left just Russ and Marielle in the large room.

Russ began walking around to all the stations to make sure the programs were closed and the computers properly shut off.

He sat at one of the machines, feeling the heat of Marielle's stare on his back, like an annoying sunburn, even though she was across the room.

"No, I don't want to talk about it," he said, not turning around as he spoke. "You've heard everything worth hearing."

"I doubt that. If you don't want to tell me any more, that's up to you. But now that everyone is gone, I wanted to thank you for being so open with them. Today, you gave them more motivation than I ever could."

He turned around in the chair. "That's not true. They like you a lot, and they're very loyal to you. They trust you completely. Rags-to-riches stories like mine are a dime a dozen. Except I'm not rich. So that probably lessens the effectiveness of anything I can say."

"Not true. Rich is in the eye of the beholder. In their eyes, you're rich. I'm sure that when you were their age, if you had seen some single guy with an expensive, trendy vehicle like yours, fashionable clothes that obviously didn't come from the local discount store or the consignment shop, and a nice house, you would have thought the same thing."

"You don't know about my house. You've never seen my house."

"I'll bet it's got about fourteen hundred square feet with two bathrooms, a double garage and a backyard with trees — although not a garden. You work too much to have a cat or a dog, but I'll bet you have some other kind of pet. Probably something exotic, although not a bird. They're too noisy and would probably annoy you. Tropical fish?"

Russ was stunned at her insight. She was right on all counts, except for the fish. "Actually, I have a lizard. A Bearded Dragon. His name is Fred."

"Ew."

"He's quiet, he doesn't smell and he's quite pleasant to hold. He's actually very gentle."

"What do you feed something like that?"

"Actually, he has a varied diet. I buy him special reptile food in a jar, he likes broccoli and some lettuces, but mostly he eats live bugs."

"Ew."

"Will you quit saying that? Fred is a great pet. Better than a cat or dog."

"Ugh! You're so frustrating! I don't want to talk about pets! I was trying to thank you! You were telling the kids about accepting help and charity and now you're refusing to accept it when all I'm trying to do is give you a compliment!"

"Calm down. You're shouting."

Her footsteps echoed on the tile floor as she walked determinedly toward him. She stopped and looked down at him as he sat in the chair. "I'm not shouting," she said through her teeth.

From the exaggerated rise and fall of her chest, Russ had a feeling she was going to chastise him. He didn't like her superior position as she hovered over him, so he turned the tables and stood, looking down at her.

She cleared her throat, her eyes flashing. "Thank you for everything you said earlier. Now just say 'you're welcome' and accept the compliment. We have to lock up."

Russ couldn't respond. This wasn't a reaction he'd experienced before when someone found out his background, nor was it a reaction he had expected. She didn't appear shocked, nor did she feel sorry for him. In fact, she was mad at him. He didn't want her sympathy, but he didn't want her anger, either.

Although, her anger was making his heart pound and his pulse race. . . .

She'd just accepted him the way he was, warts and all, and moved on. She wasn't condescending in any way, nor was she judgmental. Now that she knew that he was an older version of the kids in her under-privileged mentor group, nothing had changed. She didn't think less of his ability, or respect him any less.

He'd never met anyone like her in his life.

His own anger dissolved completely. Slowly, he raised one hand and touched her cheek with his fingertips, needing to touch her, almost to convince himself that she was real — that this was really happening and he wasn't dreaming.

"You're welcome," he said softly.

As soon as the words were out of his mouth, he could see her posture become less tense, and at the same time, her face tipped just a bit to lean her cheek into his palm.

"That's better," she whispered.

Her skin was soft. Smooth. Delicate. A

wisp of hair brushed his fingers when she moved. It was soft, too, only a different kind of soft than her skin. Like a cloud.

He gently slid his hand a couple of inches back, caressing her cheek, and then dipped the ends of his fingers into the red of her hair. That bit of red had piqued his interest from the first moment he'd seen it. The texture of it was fluffy, almost like air, but it had density.

As he caressed Marielle's hair, her eyes closed.

Something inside him snapped.

He lowered his head just a little. "You're *very* welcome," he murmured, then lowered his head completely. At first he just brushed her lips gently with his, but when he did, she made a little noise and his brain stopped functioning.

His hand closed around what he knew was the red lock of her hair, and he pressed his other hand into the small of her back, pulling her so close against him that he could feel her heart pounding. He angled his head and kissed her fully, with all the emotions he'd been holding back for so long, ever since the day he'd taken her out for dinner and they'd bantered over the bill.

He altered his stance to stand with his legs farther apart so he could hold her even closer, nestling her completely in his embrace.

He'd never in his life felt like this when he kissed a woman.

The only reason he stopped kissing her was that he needed air.

The kiss may have been over, but he wasn't ready to let her go. He didn't move as he cradled her head against his chest, enjoying the closeness. He'd never met anyone like Marielle before.

"This isn't going to work," she said into his chest.

Russ's thoughts and emotions exploded in a million directions. One of the first things he'd said to her when they first met at the hospital was that he was too busy to date. When his assigned month at the youth center was over — and it was already half over — he would be back into his normal routine, and with any luck, he would be working even more if he got the new vice president's position. He'd already acknowledged that he didn't have time to establish a relationship with a woman. He would have even less time in the future.

"I know," he whispered into her ear.

When her hair shifted at the faint movement of air with his words, he leaned his cheek into the hair resting on his palm.

Though it was the end of the day, he wanted to smell some kind of pretty, feminine shampoo, but he didn't. He didn't know where such a thought came from, but it left him sadly disappointed when there was nothing fragrant to breathe in. Although, in a way it was a good thing, because, despite what they were agreeing on, he wanted to kiss her again.

"I'm not good at this kind of thing," she said, still talking into his chest.

"That's okay. Neither am I," he said into her hair. He raised his head, spread his fingers and let the soft wisps float down like fine sand through an hourglass.

As if she felt the release, she backed up a step.

He suddenly felt cold, like a rush of frigid air had settled between them.

"It's time to close up. You go first, so I can lock the door. I guess I'll see you tomorrow, same time, same place."

Words failed him. He simply nodded and stepped outside the door. It closed behind him before he had a chance to turn around.

Tomorrow it would indeed be the same time and same place, but everything else would be different.

CHAPTER NINE

"Where did all these kids come from?" Russ asked as he looked around the room, which was getting crowded.

Marielle didn't need Russ to ask the question. She was already asking it herself. Her heart pounded. Every day they'd had a few more people than the day before, but for the first time, she was unable to count how many teens were in the youth center. There was simply too many to count without everyone being seated.

"I don't know. This is like that commercial, where one person tells two friends, and they tell two friends."

"And so on, and so on, and so on," Russ finished off for her. "We have to get more chairs. I know where they are. I'll be right back."

Marielle found it interesting that he'd automatically teamed them up as "we." It wouldn't be much longer before she would be back to being just herself, with Russ coming in as an occasional volunteer when necessary. If he remembered his promise, that is. She'd had many other people over the past two years say the same thing, only they never came back. But something deep inside her told her that Russ was good for every promise he made, and that he would be back.

She watched him as he disappeared through the door and into the main hallway.

She reminded herself, not for the first time, that the dedication and driving work ethic she found so admirable in Russ was also the thing that she disliked the most. She worked hard, too, but for different reasons. She knew what it was like to be cast aside, and she didn't want any of these teens to be cast aside just for being born on the wrong side of the tracks.

Russ returned with a dolly holding a stack of half a dozen chairs. He tipped it to set the chairs on the floor and pulled the dolly out from under them, then turned to a group of boys. "Hey! David! Get these set up, okay?" The second David acknowledged him, Russ disappeared again.

Marielle's knees began to quiver. Yesterday Russ had kissed her so sweetly she had thought she would melt.

Yes, she liked him. But she refused to make the mistake of falling in love with someone else who was going to leave her crying and feeling like a beaten puppy because she didn't have the right corporate image, and refused to make having the right corporate image her life's mission.

Her mission was right here. Instead of a tailored suit made of fine fabrics that could only be dry-cleaned, Marielle wore well-used jeans, a T-shirt from a Christian band that had been in town about five years ago, and sneakers that had seen better days. She was right where she wanted to be. Among kids who could someday be presidents and vice presidents, if only they could get a good break, or work hard enough to make their own breaks.

The door opened and Russ came in with six more chairs. This time David had dragged his friend Matt to the door with him, and they were ready and waiting. Russ set the second set of chairs down, and disappeared into the hallway once more.

He returned empty-handed, having delivered enough chairs for the newcomers, and put the dolly back in the closet.

David pointed to one of the chairs. "The seat part is loose on that one. It looks like the screws are falling out."

"I have a tool kit in my car. I'll be right back."

Russ walked to his usual computer, reached into the corner beside the monitor — and froze. He scanned the counter, then turned quickly and looked out the window, straight at his ever-shiny SUV, parked in the same spot he always used. Marielle could see his chest expand and relax in a sigh of relief. He rested his fists on his hips, his brows crinkled and his mouth tightened as he stood in one spot, obviously thinking.

"Marielle, have you seen my keys?" he called over his shoulder.

Marielle joined him so she wouldn't have to raise her voice. "Have you tried your pocket? That's where most people put their keys."

"Not true. Women put their keys in their purses."

Marielle shook her head. "Not this woman. I don't take the chance that if someone steals my purse, then along with my wallet and credit cards, they also have my keys, they know where I live, and know I'm stranded for a couple hours, unable to get home. My keys are always in my pocket." To prove her point, she reached into her back pocket, pulled them out and jingled them in his face. She also kept her keys in her pocket because she locked her purse in the desk, and needed the keys to get her purse out.

"I never put my keys in my pocket. They make my pants hang funny."

Marielle looked down. As he did every day, Russ worse loose-fitting khaki pants, never jeans. She supposed he did have a point about the weight. He also never put his cell phone in his pocket; it was always clipped to his belt.

She noticed that even though he constantly left his keys lying around, the cell phone was never off the clip unless he was using it.

"Do you think you accidentally locked them in the car? I've done that. All it took was once, though, and it never happened again."

"Impossible. I have a remote lock. I always lock it with the remote from outside." He turned and smiled at her.

Something in Marielle's stomach fluttered, making her think that she shouldn't have skipped lunch.

"You see, I've locked my keys in my car, too. And all it took was once for it never to happen again."

David joined them. "Sorry, I don't see your keys anywhere, Russ."

Marielle scanned the room, where groups of teens stood in circles talking.

"Okay. It's time to get serious," she said.

She walked behind the desk and pulled out the chair, but instead of sitting, she climbed up and stood on it. She clapped twice, then waved her hands in the air above her head. "Attention, everyone!" she called out. "We're missing a set of keys! Can everybody look around and also check your pockets? If you've got two sets of keys in there, one of them isn't yours!"

"That was subtle," Russ muttered beside her.

She looked down at him from her perch. "But it was effective. You'll notice everyone is looking."

"Maybe. Let's see what happens." He extended one hand to help her down, but all she did was stare at it.

Over a week ago, he'd clasped her hand. It had made her all tingly then, when all they were doing was arguing about who was going to pay the bill at the restaurant. It was totally innocent, but it was something she would remember for the rest of her life. She'd read all about the electricity that passed when two would-be partners touched for the first time in romance novels, but she'd never believed it really happened.

Until it happened to her.

She didn't want to touch him again, in case she got a repeat performance.

Instead, she rested one hand on the back of the chair to steady herself and began extending one foot downward. But as she shifted her weight and leaned on her hand with the back of the chair supporting her, the chair began to tip.

She drew in a sharp breath as she felt herself starting to go down. In that split second, Russ's hands clamped firmly around her waist.

The front legs of the chair settled back onto the floor, but instead of releasing her, Russ increased the pressure and lifted her down.

Her feet may have been firmly on the floor, but Marielle wasn't sure she could stand. She looked up into Russ's face because she couldn't look away.

She wanted to kiss him.

And judging from his dazed eyes and slightly parted lips, he wanted to kiss her, too.

"No one's watching," he whispered in a husky voice that made her heart beat faster.

"Not now, but it won't take much and they will be," she whispered back.

One corner of his mouth tipped up in a

lopsided grin, and one eyebrow quirked. "It's okay. It doesn't matter if anyone's watching. I just saved your life. It's to be expected."

She wanted to tell him that a couple of weeks ago, *she* had been the one to save *him,* for real. She knew now that God had put her in the right place at the right time. But the words wouldn't come out.

"Forget it," she grumbled, and stepped back.

He released her with the movement, but the impish grin remained.

Unfortunately, as they waited, no one came forward with an unclaimed set of keys.

Marielle checked her watch. "We really should get started. I'm sure they'll turn up later, when we have more time to look."

He glanced around the room, and she expected him to argue with her, but he said, "I guess. We should come up with a plan."

"A plan?"

"I can't expect all these new people to jump into the program now when we're halfway through. How about if I take the ones that have been with us all along, I'll sit on that table, and you take all the new ones that have been here less than a week and sit at the other table."

Marielle gulped. "You mean you want me

to teach them the program? I don't know it well enough for that."

"But you know the basics, and you know everything we've done so far. So you know all you need to know for today."

Marielle felt both proud that he thought so much of her abilities, and terrified. Except they didn't have a choice.

"Okay. Let's do it."

They divided the group and proceeded just as Russ had suggested. Marielle surprised herself: Russ was right. She did know enough to show the basics of the tutorial.

Russ finished his session first, but he waited until Marielle was done with her group and then called for the doughnut break, as she'd planned. Except today, she had been going to cancel the break because she knew she hadn't bought enough. But after they prayed, as she'd planned, Marielle thought she'd experienced a miracle like the New Testament story of the five loaves and two fishes, because there were enough doughnuts for everyone, and even some left over. She later overheard that Russ had sent David out to buy more while the tutorials were in session.

The same general confusion and crowd dynamics happened while they paused, and it was a relief to get the teens back to the computer tables. Yet, six o'clock came quickly, and then the group slowly filtered out, but this time, for the first time, Marielle was glad when they were all gone.

She sank down into the chair behind the desk. "I can't believe what just happened. Most of them brought a guest, but for those who didn't, someone else brought three. I'm exhausted. How are you doing?"

Russ pulled up one of the chairs, turned it backwards and sat, straddling it. "I'm fine."

Marielle leaned back in her chair, letting her head fall back. In the positions they were in, if he looked at her he would be looking straight up her nose. She was so tired she didn't care. "Are you really? Are you still getting those headaches?"

"Yes, but they're not as bad, and not as often. It's going just like my doctor told me. I expect to be all better by the time I go back to work."

"What about your memory of the accident?" she asked. "Do you remember anything yet?"

"No. But sometimes a flash of something hits me. When I try to get it back, that's when I can feel a headache coming on. So I tried to tell myself that if I ever remember, in time, it will just have to happen naturally — I can't force myself to remember. Either that or I'm psychosomatic."

"I don't think it's that at all. I know it's probably hard, but I do think you should try to let it go, and if it comes back, it will come back in its own time."

"Easier said than done." Russ stood and righted the chair. "I had better start shutting all the computers off, and make a last check for my keys, although I don't think we'll have any better results."

"Do you have an extra key for your car? Or whatever you call it? I mean, it's an SUV, but it feels silly to keep saying SUV instead of the word 'car.'"

He sighed. "In the city it's just a big car with really bad gas mileage. I do have an extra key, but it's at home, and I can't get into my house without my keys, either."

"Surely you have an extra house key."

"Yup. It's in my SUV."

Marielle sat straight and stared at him. "Any other time, I'd laugh."

"Same." He sighed and began walking toward his old computer. "I guess I'd better get started. If you wouldn't mind giving me a ride home, then I'll just have to break a window. If the cops come, I can . . . Hey . . ."

"What?"

A faint jingle sounded. "Here they are.

Right here, beside my computer, exactly where I left them."

"Well, don't you feel embarrassed?"

He turned around, holding his keys in front of him. "No. They were definitely not there before. It wasn't just me, either. When you so delicately asked everyone to look around, a number of the kids checked out the tables. If they were here, one of them would have noticed."

"Then that's really strange." Marielle shrugged. "I guess someone must have scooped them into their pocket after all, and then been too embarrassed to admit it."

"I guess. But it would have set my mind at ease a lot sooner if they had have said something. Mistakes happen. I could have lived with it."

"Well, what's done is done. Now let's get everything packed up and get out of here. I'm going to bed early tonight."

They packed up in silence and left quickly.

Marielle was never so glad to get home. Tonight, instead of supper, she had only the energy to make herself some toast with peanut butter. She even was going to skip her evening cup of tea and go straight to bed.

Just as the toast popped out of the toaster, the phone rang.

"Marielle, it's me. Russ. If you can, I need you to come over to my house as soon as you can get here. Get a pen and I'll give you directions."

CHAPTER TEN

Russ paced the floor, unable to sit still.

He didn't even wait for the doorbell to ring. The second she turned off her engine, he opened the door. He could tell the exact moment she saw him. She froze, then, instead of walking, she jogged up the sidewalk. He stepped backward to give her room to get into the hallway, closing the door once she was inside.

"What's wrong?" she panted.

"Someone broke into my house while I was at the youth center today."

She pressed both hands over her mouth. "Oh, no! What was stolen?" she gasped.

Russ ran his fingers through his hair. "That's the strange thing. Nothing."

Her hands drifted down. "That's good. I guess you scared them off when you got home."

He swept one hand in the air in the direction of his neighbor's house. "No. I didn't.

The neighbors told me that my alarm went off about an hour and a half ago. They didn't see anything. They said there wasn't a strange car parked on the street or in my driveway, they didn't see anyone hanging around, and since there weren't any open windows they didn't call the cops — they thought it was a false alarm. The only reason they phoned me was to complain about the noise."

Marielle drew her hands into balls and rested her fists on her hips. "That's awful! But at least your neighbors scared them off. How much damage was done to your house?"

"None, actually."

Her head tipped to one side. "Let me get this straight. Nothing was stolen, no damage was done to your house, and the neighbors didn't see anyone."

"That's right. But I know someone was here. Because of the computer. The keyboard isn't where I left it. I always push it forward when I'm done because I hot-sync my PDA every time I power it down. That way what I've finished working on is backed up. But when I got home, after the neighbors told me the alarm had gone off, the first thing I did after I made sure Fred was okay was run in here to see if someone stole my computer. It wasn't stolen, but it definitely had been used. It was properly turned off, but someone had turned it on and was using it while they were here."

"That doesn't make any sense."

"I know. But that doesn't negate the fact that it happened."

"How do you know for sure?"

"I have my e-mail program loaded so it opens on start-up and downloads my new messages. When I turned it on, there were messages on it that I hadn't read, and the time they were downloaded was about the same as when my neighbor said the alarm went off."

"But that doesn't make any sense. You'd think if someone broke in, they would turn everything to be marked as unread to cover their tracks."

"I'm guessing they were in a rush and didn't want to take the time with the alarm blaring."

"But what about a password? If you work from home sometimes, don't you need to keep your computer secure?"

"No. When I work from home, I network up into the company's server. For that, I need a password. But it's a pain to have to log in with a password every time I log in to my own computer at home, just for personal stuff. Do you set a password to log in to your home computer?"

"Well . . . No . . ."

"See?"

"Never mind that. Have you called the police?"

He ran his fingers through his hair again. "Yes. But there was no sign of forced entry, nothing was stolen, and no one saw anything, so they told me it would be pointless to come down."

"Are you sure? Maybe some friend or relative was here to see you, and they used your computer while they were waiting, but you didn't show up by the time they had to go."

"That's not likely. No one has a key except my mother, and she doesn't live in town. She also knows my security code. There wasn't a car in the driveway. Anyone I know would park in the driveway and knock on the door. As well, anyone who knew me would phone me on my cell phone for the code to shut off the alarm, not just let it scream until it automatically reset. No one called. But you're right about the key. That's the only way someone could get in quickly without breaking a lock or a window. Remember when my keys were missing this afternoon? I think someone took them, came here, checked out my place, then put the keys back, hoping I wouldn't notice they were gone."

"That's ridiculous."

"But it's the only way this could have happened. There were lots of people there we didn't know, and for most of the time, everyone was milling around freely. It would have been easy to scoop up my keys, and just as easy to put them back later." He turned and stared at his computer. "It just doesn't make sense that someone would go to all that trouble and then leave without taking anything. It would have been the perfect crime."

"Why did you ask me to come?"

"If someone had my keys, they could have made copies. The only thing that they couldn't have duplicated was the key to my SUV — that has to be obtained at the dealer. But for everything else . . ." He sighed. "I don't want to leave the house again thinking someone could wait for me to go, and then waltz in with a key. After one apparent false alarm, if it happened a second time, my neighbors wouldn't even look to see if anything was going on. I want someone to be here while I go to the hardware store. I'm going to change all the locks tonight, including the lock on my shed in the backyard where I keep my lawn mower and stuff." He stilled. "I actually never looked in the shed. I wonder if everything is still in there, since everything in the house is apparently intact . . ."

Then he shook his head. "No. My neighbor didn't see anything, and he surely would have noticed someone going down the street with a lawn mower. Would you mind staying here while I go to the hardware store? You can watch television, or I have a bunch of DVDs — you can watch a movie if I've got anything you haven't seen."

"Sure. I can stay."

"Great." He checked his watch. "I have to go now. The only place that's open right now is going to close in half an hour. Make yourself at home. I'll be back as soon as I can."

He left the house and drove to the home center discount store as quickly as possible without getting a speeding ticket. Following the list he'd made of all the locks in his house, he filled the buggy with everything he needed and was on his way to the checkout, but at the end of the aisle, he skidded to a halt.

Against the wall was the key-cutting booth.

He stared at it for a couple of seconds, steeled his nerve, then approached the young clerk, who was slouched in a tall chair, over-chewing her gum and reading a book. "Excuse me. Can you tell me if anyone was in here about two hours ago to get a bunch of keys made?"

She snapped her gum and looked at him like he was daft. "Lots of people come in here to get keys made, mister."

"No. I mean like more than one."

"Yeah. Lots of people."

He tried to tamp his frustration, which was already near his limit. "But did anyone come in here tonight and ask for a copy of three different keys at the same time."

"Probably."

Russ pulled his key chain out of his pocket and laid it on the counter. "Does this particular set of keys look familiar? Did anyone come in and get copies of these ones?"

She picked up the key chain, ran her fingers over his house key, the shed key and the key that led from the garage into the house. She then poked at the antique car key-chain fob his sister had given him. "Yeah. I seen these here before. Nice car."

"Can you describe the person who had the keys made?"

"Mister, I get, like, a dozen people an hour. I can't remember everyone."

Russ didn't mention that since he'd been there, not a single other person had requested a key made. "Let's start with the basics, then. Was the person male or female."

She snapped the gum again. "Female."

For some reason, Russ found that odd, but stranger things had happened. "Can you describe her?"

"I see too many people each night to do that."

Russ knew that by arguing, he would lose any advantage he had. "Then do you remember what color hair she had?"

"Nope."

"What she was wearing?"

"I'm not the fashion police. I just make keys. You want more of those, I can do that. But ya gotta hurry. We, like, close in five minutes. I need a couple of minutes."

Russ picked up his key chain. "No, enough copies were made as it is. Thanks for your help."

His patience continued to wear thin as he waited in line along with the other last-minute shoppers. He tried to remember all the girls who had been at the youth center. He knew some a little, but he didn't know them all, and those whom he did know, he didn't know well.

He certainly didn't understand why some-one would go to such trouble just to use his computer, although now that he had pur-chased the new locks, he could take the time to try to figure out what the girl who had invaded his home was doing on his com-puter. The first thing he intended to do was check to see if she'd gone to any porno Web sites, and next, he would call up a complete history and see if his name had been entered or mentioned anywhere.

The possibilities for theft were endless. He also would have to see if anything he'd purchased online had allowed her to access his credit card number in his system's cache. He was always careful about the number, but it was just his home computer, so sometimes at home he got sloppy. If that happened, he worried that he'd have a ter-rible charge bill at the end of the month.

With each possibility that entered his mind, the checkout line seemed to go more and more slowly. By the time he paid for his new locks, he was so anxious to get home that he ran through the parking lot to his SUV. This time, he drove home knowing he was going too fast, but he couldn't slow down. If his credit card was stored in his computer's memory, he had to find out and stop any transactions.

He only hoped that if anything had been done, the girl who had done it had carelessly entered her own name and address. Then, he would have his perpetrator, caught red-handed.

When he walked to his door, bag in hand, the front door was locked, which was good. He didn't have a dog to bark when a stranger came to the door, so if the girl dared to come back, at least Marielle would hear the lock being opened and be able to do something.

Russ felt too strange about knocking on his own door, so he used his key — the last time he would ever use that particular key.

Marielle wasn't waiting for him, nor did she call out his name to make sure it was him who was coming in.

Russ hurried to the living room. He opened his mouth to call her, but at the last second, he snapped it shut.

The television was playing quietly, a cup of tea rested on a magazine on the coffee table, and Marielle was lying on his couch, fast asleep.

With his lizard lying on her stomach, also sleeping.

The woman had made herself at home, just like he'd said.

He set the bag containing the new locks

down on the coffee table as gently as he could, hoping not to make any noise.

He didn't often have people over to his house. He was usually too busy to make much in the way of plans. Sometimes he went out with his friends, but most evenings he was too tired after a long day at work, so he simply stayed home alone. But Marielle was obviously comfortable. She even looked like she belonged there.

Many times, Russ had wondered what it would be like to have a wife, someone who would be there when he got home; someone who would share his life, and whose life he could share in return. Someone he would just be happy to sit and spend time with, without the need to talk — just being together would be good enough.

But it wasn't going to happen. He was nearly thirty, too old for such ridiculous fantasies. Real life wasn't like that. He had his career and all its demands. One day he might settle down, but first he would make sure all loose ends were tied up, and there would never, ever be the chance that he could lose it all — the way his mother had. He would never put anyone through what he went through, adult or child.

Marielle made a soft snore, then settled back down into deep, even breathing. Fred continued to lie on her stomach, not moving.

Russ crossed his arms and watched the two of them.

Not that he dated much, but not a single woman he'd ever gone out with had touched his lizard, never mind picked Fred up and had a nap with him.

He remembered Marielle's reaction when he told her that he had a lizard for a pet. He liked that she hadn't stuck to her preconceived ideas, and that she trusted him enough to check Fred out without condemning the lizard.

Just like she didn't condemn him.

He approached her and bent down to retrieve his lizard, but stopped short. His fingers would definitely brush her as he reached beneath the lizard's stomach to pick him up. He didn't want to invade her space by touching her when she was unaware of his presence.

"Marielle? Wake up. I'm back."

Her eyes fluttered open. She began to move like she was going to sit up, but as soon as she became aware of her surroundings, she rested one hand on the lizard and lay back down.

"I'm so embarrassed. I don't know how I fell asleep. I guess you can tell that curiosity got the best of me and I picked up your lizard."

Russ smiled. "He likes you. You must be a good heat source."

He couldn't help it, but in addition to Fred, Russ liked her, too. In fact, he was starting to worry that he liked her far too much, something that hurt because she was right — it would never work between them. He was at a turning point in his career. From the day he turned sixteen and got his first job, he'd nearly killed himself to get to the point he was at now — and his future hinged on what he did in the next three weeks. The last thing he needed was a relationship.

She pressed one hand to Fred's back to support him, pushed herself to a sitting position, then stood. "Did you get what you needed?"

"Yes. Since Fred doesn't bark when he hears a noise, I'm going to start changing the locks right now, the front door first. The thing is that now, I'm going to have a different key for every door in the house, instead of being able to use the same key for all three doors. But it can't be helped. I have to use hardware store locks because I refuse to pay for a night call to a locksmith. I usually only use the front door and the door leading to the garage anyway."

"I live in a town house. I only have one key. The back is a patio door that only locks from the inside. Since I'm here, would you like me to hold a flashlight or anything?"

He retrieved his tools from the shed while Marielle tucked Fred back in his habitat, and they met at the front door.

"I found out from the clerk at the key booth that it was a girl who was here. That narrows the list of suspects, but any possible reason escapes me."

"I'm just so shocked any of my girls would do such a thing. I trusted all of them. But then there have been a bunch of them this last week that I don't know. The more I think about it, the more it bothers me. I don't even know how anyone in the group, even the core group, would know where you live. Not that they couldn't look you up in the phone book, but I never told any of them your last name."

Russ nearly dropped the screw. "You're right. I certainly never told anyone my last name. It's not important to them. They all address me by my first name. I think I would faint if anyone called me Mr. Branson." He mentally shuddered. The nurse at the hospital had called him Mr. Branson. That experience alone could give him nightmares for the rest of his life.

"Tomorrow we'll have to watch all the girls and see if we think any of them was missing for an hour in the middle. It complicates things that we split up into two groups. Just because someone wasn't in my group doesn't mean they were gone. They were probably in your group. Everybody but one."

They didn't talk much while they changed the four locks. Russ didn't want to change the lock to the shed in the dark, but he didn't have to worry too much about someone tiptoeing into the shed in the middle of the night. He could do it in the morning.

They were nearly done when his stomach grumbled noisily. He felt himself blush so intensely that the burn extended all the way to his ears. "I haven't had supper. When I discovered what happened I wanted to take care of all the details fast. And now that I think about it, you probably haven't had supper, either. Can I make you something?"

"I actually helped myself to some toast while you were gone. You said to make myself at home. I hope you don't mind."

"Of course I don't mind, except that toast isn't supper. I can fire up the barbecue and make us a couple of burgers in a few minutes. Interested?"

"I really should be going. I have to get up early."

"Won't that nap help? I'm cooking anyway."

She stared at him. He didn't want to beg, but he was ready to start thinking of more reasons she should stay.

He wanted her to stay.

Needed her to stay.

But having her stay was such a bad idea. He didn't want to start something he couldn't finish, and he couldn't finish anything with Marielle.

"Burgers sound like a great idea, but only if I can help."

Relief washed through him. "Deal."

To eat faster, he defrosted a couple of patties in the microwave, then went outside to cook them while Marielle cut up a tomato and fried an onion.

He had just flipped the burgers the first time when the patio door slid open behind him.

"I just thought of something," she said.

He turned around to see Marielle poised behind him, holding his biggest knife, the tip pointed skyward.

"If it was anyone else holding that knife like that, I'd be nervous."

Her cheeks turned to a charming shade of

pink, and she lowered the blade. "Do you remember the other day when one of the computers was left on at the center, when we were positive they had all been shut off? Do you think someone got into the church unauthorized, too?"

"That's interesting. And highly possible. Have your keys ever gone missing for a short period of time?"

"Never. My keys are always either in my pocket, or in my hand." She turned and walked back into the house before he could respond.

The computer that had been on was his old one from the office. Now someone had been into his computer at home. He had no idea what anyone might want on either computer. He certainly didn't do online shopping at the youth center, nor had he ever used his personal credit card at work.

His first instinct was to change the passwords on the computers at the center. The only people who were supposed to know the password were himself, Marielle and Pastor Tom, and in just over a week, it would be only Marielle and Pastor Tom.

He flipped the burgers again. Again, the patio door opened behind him.

"I thought of something else. If someone is trying to steal programs, we should check the box in the corner at the center tomorrow and make sure everything is still there. Those programs cost a lot of money, even if they're not the latest versions."

"Good idea. I think these are ready. Are you done in there?"

"Yes. You have a very nice kitchen for a man."

"Do you mean that I have a nice kitchen with lots of stuff that's designed for a man, or I have a nice kitchen despite the fact that I'm a man."

"Uh . . ."

He laughed. "It's okay. I like to eat, so it only makes sense that I like to cook." And now, he could afford to cook anything he wanted to eat, in contrast to when he was growing up, dividing a box of generic-brand macaroni-and-cheese so it could feed three people for supper, when none of them had eaten lunch.

They prepared their buns, but when they were ready to take first bites, instead of eating, Marielle folded her hands together on the table and looked up at him with expectant eyes.

She wanted him to pray.

He hadn't prayed for years, especially not out loud. He'd asked God many questions, but he hadn't actually prayed.

He looked down at his burger.

He had lots of things to be thankful for. The most obvious — a good job. A good home. Friends. A gas guzzler for a vehicle — but it was almost new, trendy, and it had been his choice to buy it.

He glanced at Marielle. He wanted to add her to his list of friends, but she was certainly more than a friend, yet not a friend at all. They'd spent a lot of time together, and the better he came to know her, the more he liked her. But they couldn't continue this thing, whatever it was, when his "volunteer" time at the center was over.

Still, for now, he had a lot of things to be thankful for. Not the least of which was the reason he had met Marielle in the first place.

He was alive and mobile. Sometimes, what was important simply came down to basics.

Russ folded his hands on the table and bowed his head. "Dear Lord, thank You for this good food, and that we're here together, safe and sound. Amen."

She paused, giving him the impression she had been expecting him to say more, but finally she answered with a soft "Amen."

They took their first bites simultaneously.

"That wasn't so hard after all, was it?"

He smiled. "No. It wasn't." Actually, it had been pretty easy. It had also felt good.

"Now that the panic is over, I wanted to thank you for coming over so quickly."

"You're welcome." She smiled. "That was pretty easy, too."

"Point taken. I hope finding out who is behind breaking into my house will also be easy. Even though nothing was broken and nothing was taken, I feel violated. My personal space has been invaded, and there was nothing I could have done to stop it. Although, I suppose instead of just having a noisy alarm, I should have gone the extra mile and gotten a monitored system. Then the police would have come."

"Hindsight is always twenty-twenty."

After finishing her burger, Marielle stood. "I hate to be rude and rush off, but I'm really tired. I think I should get home and get to bed."

Russ stood as well. "Don't worry about the mess, I'm just going to throw everything in the dishwasher."

Once at the door he reached forward to wrap his hand around the doorknob, but he didn't turn it. "This feels really strange. I should be escorting you home, not throwing you out the door."

"I came on my own. I can certainly get home on my own."

"I know you can. I just wanted to end the

evening right." He shuffled closer, making it clear without actually having to say it that he wanted to kiss her good-night.

She looked up at him, studying his face.

"Okay," she said, her lips curving into the most delicate of smiles. "Close your eyes."

His eyes drifted shut in glorious anticipation. She picked up both his hands, including the one on the doorknob, and wrapped her tiny hands around his.

Her touch made his heart beat double time.

"Good night," she whispered huskily.

He held his breath, waiting.

Her lips brushed his cheek, then settled in for a loud popping smooch.

"See you tomorrow," she said quickly.

The door opened and closed behind her before he had a chance to open his eyes.

CHAPTER ELEVEN

"Can I bring the doughnuts tomorrow? Actually, we should alternate days."

"That's a kind offer, but you don't have to do this, you know."

"I know that. But I want to. Indulge me."

Marielle stared up at Russ. She'd almost indulged him last night. He'd made it more than obvious that he wanted to kiss her. And she had kissed him — only not the way he wanted.

Oh, but the man could kiss, especially for someone who claimed that he didn't date much. The few dates he went on must have been something that would jump off the page of a woman's journal.

Yet as much as she sensed he wanted to move forward, she also sensed a hesitation.

She also had her own reasons for hesitating. When both of them were unsure of the wisdom of what they were doing, that was enough of a reason to stop.

Together they turned to watch Jason digging through the box of program CDs. Russ lowered his head so he could talk softly enough not to be overheard by others. "Jason hasn't said any of the programs are missing, and all the computers were still off when we got here, so everything must be fine. At the same time, after my keys going missing, I'm still nervous."

Brittany walked to the desk. "Marielle, where are the disks you had here with the stuff to make the brochures? I need one."

Marielle quickly joined Brittany at the desk, not that she expected Brittany to be wrong. She opened the drawers, just in case, but they weren't there, either. "Russ! All the disks are gone! The whole pile of them!"

He strode to her side. "I don't understand. Didn't you say that all you had on them was clip art and digital images?"

"Yes. Every one of them was the same, too. But they were here last night. I think." She bowed her head and pressed her fingers to her temples. "I can't remember at what point I lost track of them. I remember knocking over the stack shortly after I got here, but I don't remember if the stack was on the desk when we locked up."

"I know. We were too busy talking about my keys. This could be unrelated."

"Or it could be *very* related."

Russ turned around slowly, looking at all the windowsills, which were just below eye level for him because he was so tall. "I don't see anything amiss in the dust patterns. No one has come in or out through the windows. They must have disappeared during the session."

Brittany turned to her. "Is something wrong?" she asked.

Marielle turned to her. "We're not sure. I don't know if I forgot where I put the disks, or if someone took them. But it doesn't look like anyone broke in, and there was nothing important on them, so I must have just left them somewhere."

Brittany shrugged, then walked across the room to sit at the computer next to Jason.

Marielle's eyes met Russ's across the room. She took that to acknowledge their nonverbal agreement that both of them would keep an eye on all the girls present, first and foremost, to try to determine if any one of them went missing for any amount of time, and second, to find out if any of the girls knew Russ's last name.

When they split into two groups to continue with their projects, Marielle paid far more attention to everyone in her group rather than focusing on the program. She either knew each step, or she didn't.

This time when they took the break for the doughnuts, Marielle kept an attentive eye on the door.

No one came in, no one left.

When they were done with the tutorials, all the teens gathered in small circles to chat. Marielle watched the group from one side of the room, Russ from the other. But everyone behaved completely normally. It made Marielle almost feel like she'd imagined everything.

After the teens left, Russ followed his usual routine. "I think I know who our mystery nonthief might be," he said as he began powering down the first computer. "I don't know her name, but that girl with the blue T-shirt and pierced nose was acting really strange. Jumpy. She was nervous about something."

"Okay. We'll both keep an eye on her tomorrow. Now let's make sure everything is locked up."

This time, Russ left extra early in order to arrive at the church before Marielle.

It was Friday.

Double-duty day.

This time he didn't say more than a simple greeting to Pastor Tom when he opened the door. Today, Russ had other things to think about. Like catching the culprit.

He set about checking the room carefully, and not in a rushed way as he had the day before.

His injuries were healing. Today nothing hurt when he got down on his hands and knees and checked to make sure everything was as he had left it.

He had trusted that Jason applied the metal loop attachments properly, but today, Russ wiggled and pulled on every one, just to make sure.

Everything was secure.

He looked at the time, confirming that Marielle still wasn't due for another twenty minutes, so he climbed on a chair and pushed up on the ceiling tile where he'd hidden the keys. After checking them, he stacked them in what looked to be a haphazard manner, then pulled his digital camera out of his pocket and took a picture, just so he'd know later if they'd been moved.

He also checked the locks on the windows and took a picture of every one of them from the proper angles, so the dust patterns were plainly showing.

When he was done, he unlocked the door from the inside, pending Marielle's arrival, and began his routine of turning all the computers on.

He had booted up the last one when the door opened.

He rose and turned around as he spoke. "Hey, Marielle. You're late this . . ."

"Hey, Russ. Uh . . ." When Jason saw only Russ and no Marielle, he skidded to a halt and looked around. "Where's Marielle?"

"I don't know. She's late."

"She's never late. The only time she was ever late was the day of your accident. She told us about that the day it happened. She was pretty shook up."

Russ's gut tightened.

He didn't want to think that she'd been in an accident, but she did drive through the busy downtown core every day to get here, and accidents happened all the time.

Lord, please keep her safe. The prayer zipped through his mind, surprising him. But at the same time, deep in his heart, he knew he was doing the right thing by asking God.

Russ pulled his cell phone off his belt clip and hit the button to auto-dial her number.

The door opened at the same time as a melodic ring tone began.

Russ looked up as Marielle ran through the door, fumbling with a big bag from the doughnut shop, her purse and her cell phone.

"Hello?" she muttered into the phone.

Russ blinked, trying to process her voice coming through the cell phone at the same time as he heard her live, in front of him.

"You're late," he said into the phone while watching her face.

Her eyebrows crinkled and she looked up at him.

"Not funny," she mumbled as she snapped the phone shut.

Russ also closed his phone and hooked it onto his belt clip. "I was worried about you. Where were you?"

Her eyes were haunted. "I was at the doughnut shop. While I was inside, someone broke into my car."

"What was stolen?"

She hustled across the room and set the bag of doughnuts on the desk. "That's the thing. Nothing. It was hot, so I left the window down about an inch, but someone somehow managed to unlock the door and get in. When I got back to the car, someone had gone through my glovebox and looked under the seats, because everything was a mess. But nothing seemed to be missing. But then, I don't have anything in my car worth stealing."

Russ ran his fingers through his hair. "This is getting really strange. Jason, do you know that girl who came here yesterday wearing that blue T-shirt and a blue earring in her nose?"

"Yeah. That's Tamera. Colin's sister. She's never been to anything like this and she was really nervous, but when we got home she said everything was okay and she had had a really good time. Why?"

"Oh. Never mind."

Marielle turned to Jason. "Who do you know that comes here that has a car?"

"Nobody. I know a couple of people in the group who have their license, but they don't get the car until their dads get home from work. Why?"

"I was wondering if anyone who came here might have left the group for a little while and gone out driving."

"Not that I know of. That doesn't make any sense. Why would anyone do that? This place isn't open very long, and no one wants to miss anything."

"That's good to hear. Now I have to hurry and get ready."

Russ watched as Marielle pulled a digital camera out of her purse.

"Well," he said. "That's certainly worth stealing."

"That's why it's in my purse, and I don't leave it just sitting in the car, even if I'm only gone for a couple of minutes."

He patted his own pocket, now lumpy and making his pants hang lopsided because of the weight of his own digital camera.

"We're going to get pictures of all the girls tonight."

"Don't you think that's going to cause a bit of an uproar?"

"Nope." Marielle grinned from ear to ear. "Tonight, after the supper break, I've got a guest coming who's a makeup artist. She's going to do demos on everyone, so I'll have a chance to get before and after pictures of all the girls, and any boys who choose to submit themselves."

Russ raised his eyebrows. "Boys?"

"Male movie stars wear makeup. They are just not as obvious as the girls. Some men and teenage boys are now starting to wear makeup when they want to look their best."

Jason nodded. "Yeah. I know a guy in one of my classes who wears nail polish. He just picks guy colors."

Russ didn't think there was any such thing as a "guy" color when it came to nail polish, so he thought it best to pass on that one.

"Then when we're done, we can look at

the pictures, rule out the obvious ones, and take the rest down to the person at the key booth to see if she can identify who made those keys off your key chain."

"She really wasn't very cooperative."

"It doesn't hurt to ask. The worst that can happen is she'll say no."

The usual hoard of teenagers started arriving, cutting their conversation short.

Russ watched as Marielle interacted with them. They loved her. She fit in comfortably, and when she was with them some of their slang and jargon slipped into her speech patterns. He was positive that she didn't dress like that at her workplace, yet she was completely at ease wearing casual street clothes that looked like something the kids might find cool, rather than a more stuffy outfit.

She was the picture of everything he'd worked to get out of and never look back.

Except he was looking right at her.

His world rocked on its axis.

The disparity of his goals and what was happening around him was making his ulcer act up for the first time in over a week. He reached into his pocket for his package of antacids and popped a couple in his mouth.

As much as he liked Marielle, he was making a path for himself, and that was to move forward with his life, not backward into what he once had been.

This assignment was temporary. If he chose to do so, when next week was over, he would be able to once again move ahead with his career.

Except he'd promised Marielle that he'd come back and help her when she needed him.

Words his mother taught him echoed through his head.

"But let your 'Yes' be 'Yes' and your 'No' be 'No.' Whatever is more than these is of the evil one." Matthew 5:37.

He squeezed his eyes shut. Russ had never made a promise he wouldn't or couldn't keep. And he'd promised he would teach the youth center participants computer skills.

When he sat in the chair at his old computer it didn't take long for the original group to follow him. Marielle led her group, and both took a break at the prearranged time.

This time, instead of paying for pizza, Marielle sent a couple of the boys to her car, and they returned carrying a couple of large coolers filled with sandwiches and fruit.

"Did you make all that last night after you

got home from my place?" asked Russ.

"Yes."

"No wonder you wanted to get home so fast. Why didn't you tell me? I could have helped. At the very least I could have helped you pay for it."

"I did fine. Help yourself, there's lots for everyone, including you."

Marielle waved her hands in the air to silence the group. "Let's pray, and then we'll eat!" She lowered her head and folded her hands in front of her. "Dear God, thanks for this food, for this group, and for this fine building to meet in. Amen!"

"That was short," said Russ.

"My longer prayers are for my private time with God. You know, I think the only times I've ever heard you pray was just before we eat."

"That's because I don't think it's right to pray only when you want something," he said.

"Pastor Tom told me that his Sunday message is on the power of prayer. Would you like to come? I'll bet that you learn something. Please? If you can't come for yourself, will you come for me?"

"I'll think about it."

"I'd really like it if you came with me."

"I'll let you know. Now let's eat. I have a

feeling that if we don't grab some food now, we're not going to get any."

He managed to get a sandwich, but he hadn't taken more than a couple of bites when the door opened and a woman carrying a big pink plastic tote walked in.

"Susan! I'm so glad you could make it!" Marielle exclaimed.

Susan smiled sweetly. "I'm glad to be here. Are we ready to start?"

"Yes!" Marielle gathered all the girls together, then called Russ.

"Here. Can you take our picture for a before shot?"

Russ shoveled the rest of the sandwich into his mouth and stepped back. "This isn't going to work. If we're going to see the results, I need a close-up shot of everyone for the detail. Do you ladies mind if I take individual pictures instead of a group shot?"

Those who didn't nod, shrugged, so Russ took that as a collective yes.

He snapped a close-up picture of every girl there, including Marielle when she wasn't paying attention to him. He noticed that not a single male remained at that particular table except himself, and he was only there because he'd been hijacked to be the photographer.

During the application of each layer of

makeup, Russ also snapped more pictures, hoping first that Marielle's camera had a large enough memory card to handle everything he intended to take, and second, that she had new batteries. He found the process interesting because the technique of applying the makeup was something he'd never seen before. Then, when all the girls were done, they insisted that Marielle also have a makeover.

"No. Not me. I don't wear much makeup."

Susan clapped her hands together once. "You have to do this! Giving you a makeover is one of the main reasons I came. It was fun to do all these lovely young ladies, and I need a challenge."

"A challenge?" Marielle sputtered. "I don't know if I like the sound of that."

"I mean that you're an adult, and your skin texture will be different and you'll have different needs. Let me show you."

Before Marielle could protest more, Susan had her seated in the chair and was already applying something to Marielle's cheeks.

For this, Russ swapped cameras and used his own.

When they were done, Russ's chin nearly hit the floor. The beautiful woman seated in the chair was every inch Marielle, but at the same time, she was completely different.

She was the most beautiful woman he'd seen in his life.

After the girls divided into groups to pick through Susan's samples, Susan held out a mirror to Marielle.

"This isn't me," Marielle said, staring at her reflection.

"But it is." Susan waved to Russ. "If you'll give me that camera, I'll take a picture of the two of you together."

"As long as you don't come near me with that tube of lipstick," Russ said.

"Some men are starting to wear makeup, you know."

"I heard. But not this one."

Russ rested his hands on the back of the chair where Marielle sat, bent at the waist and leaned forward so his face was next to hers. The woman took a couple of pictures, then returned the camera.

"It's time for me to go. Thanks for having me."

"Thank you for doing this, Susan. I hope someday these girls will buy your makeup," said Marielle.

"Whether they do or not doesn't matter. What does matter was that we all had fun."

After Susan left, the girls started filtering out, and when they started leaving, so did the boys who had been paying much more attention than usual.

"This was a good idea. I hope it works. When we go to the key-making booth tomorrow we just might have our answers."

"W . . . we?" Marielle stammered. "What do you mean? Why do you want me to go with you?"

"She wasn't very cooperative with me. Hopefully you'll get a better reaction."

"If you think it will make a difference, sure, I can go with you."

"I also want to take you out for lunch on the way there. You do so much for everyone else, it's about time someone did something for you, and I accept that responsibility."

At first Marielle frowned, but soon her thoughtful expression changed to an impish grin. "Okay. I'll go with you for lunch and to the home center store if you come to church with me on Sunday."

"You're kidding, right?"

"Nope. That's the deal."

"That's silly. The trip to the home center store is to benefit us both, and me buying you lunch benefits you."

"And going to church on Sunday will benefit you."

He couldn't argue with that logic. Strangely, now that he was obligated to go, he didn't mind. In fact, he was almost looking forward to returning to church after so many years.

"All right. I'll go."

Russ found himself smiling. Maybe it was time. He wasn't sure what would happen, but it seemed a good time to find out.

CHAPTER TWELVE

Russ scanned the interior of the church. Of course the inside was as old as the outside, but it was in much better condition for its age. The walls were plain and painted a neutral beige, and the ceiling appeared to be some kind of hardwood. The floor was covered by a well-worn Berber-style carpet that had seen better days. He suspected that it covered a hardwood floor that was the same wood as the ceiling, except the floor beneath was probably in worse shape than the carpet that covered it.

At the front, light shone in a rainbow of colors through the two stained-glass windows, one on each side of the raised area where sat an elaborately carved wooden podium. The wooden pews also reflected times gone by. They were worn, but clean and polished, at least where the verathane hadn't been worn off. Well-used hymnals were nestled in little pockets on the backs of the pews, giving the whole place a well-loved ambience.

In place of an organ, a small group of musicians played a contemporary Christian hymn, allowing people to talk without raising their voices before the service began.

Russ turned his head and looked behind him. Nearly every seat was filled, and in many of the pews, people were standing and shuffling in closer together to make room for others to squeeze in beside someone they knew.

Today was the first time Russ had been in the sanctuary. Until now, he'd spent most of his time in the church basement. "Wow," he muttered as he glanced around. "This place is packed."

She turned to him, rested her hand on his arm and smiled. "No more than usual for a Sunday morning."

Russ was about to tell her that he didn't know how so many people could fit into such a small place, but someone called out Marielle's name and waved, interrupting him. She waved back, then waved to a few more people in the crowd who waved to her. She even went so far as to playfully blow a kiss in the air toward one of the teenaged boys, who pretended to catch it. The boy then kissed his closed fist, and laughed before turning back to his friend.

Russ leaned his head toward her so he could speak quietly. "Do you know *everybody* here?"

"Of course not. But I do know most."

It looked like it, too. She was completely in her element, and she looked so happy she nearly glowed.

Russ didn't feel nervous about being here; in fact, the opposite was true. He felt fairly comfortable, and that was what made him nervous. He shouldn't have felt comfortable. It was just like the church his mother had taken him to when he was growing up. In fact, the building was probably the same age.

Yesterday, before he and Marielle had gone to the home center store, he'd taken her to a quaint little bistro he liked, where they were on his "turf."

He'd seen a few people he knew, and had nodded politely at them. He didn't wave at people across a crowded room. He certainly didn't blow kisses in the air.

Yet he felt more comfortable in Marielle's church than he had yesterday, where he should have been in his element.

It wasn't right.

He was a glutton for punishment.

Yesterday, he'd told himself all the reasons

they shouldn't keep seeing each other, yet here he was again, not hating the experience, but actually looking forward to maybe once again joining with other believers in God's presence.

The sad fact was that all the time he had left to be with her was one week, and then he would be back at his job. He had no good reason or opportunity to see her again unless she called him to say she was having trouble with either a program or one of the computers.

Since the worship leader still hadn't approached the podium, Marielle turned toward him.

"I can't believe that the clerk didn't recognize a single one of the girls as the one who made duplicates of your keys yesterday. What are we going to do now?"

Russ found it interesting that she had grouped them together as "we," when really, it was his problem, not hers. "I don't know. This puts us back to square one, doesn't it?"

"Not really. At least we know there's a security breach. I just wish I could find some sensible reason."

"They're teenagers. Sometimes there is no reason."

"There's always a reason. Even if it's a

stupid reason, there will be one."

Before Russ could respond, a man's voice boomed over the loudspeakers welcoming everyone present, and inviting the congregation to stand.

Russ followed along with the order of the service, feeling more and more like it had been far too long since he'd last done this very thing, though it had been his own choice. He looked up at the old, scarred cross hanging on the wall near the ceiling. It wasn't that God had turned his back on Russ. God had been faithful. Russ knew it was he who had turned his back on God.

He knew he would be back next week, with a new and improved attitude.

Without asking, when the service was over he automatically followed Marielle down to the youth center room in the basement.

Today, it was only boys in the room, taking advantage of the day that was open for the online games. Today, he didn't think about anything more than simply having a bit of good, honest fun.

Even though it had been three weeks that he'd been off work, today was the first time he could say he really felt relaxed. In the end, Grant had been right. Russ *had* needed more than a couple of days off.

Marielle's laughter destroyed his concentration and caused Russ to crash his helicopter.

He stood. "I've had enough. If anyone wants to use my player, I've got a lot of points built up."

A boy whose name he couldn't remember quickly took his chair. Russ watched the boy immediately fire up another helicopter and take off.

Marielle knew all their names, even the new ones. He still didn't know all the names of the regulars. Russ made up his mind to learn them, even if he only had a week left.

Suddenly the lunch Marielle had made and he'd so much enjoyed turned to a lump in his stomach.

One week left.

Marielle's voice rang out from the corner of the room, but there was suddenly no tone of gaiety. "Russ, can you come here, please?"

"What's up?" he asked, concerned.

"Look." Marielle pointed to the shelf in the corner of the room.

"So? It's a pile of disks."

She slid closer to him. "These are the disks that went missing a couple of days ago. I know I didn't put them here. I would never have put them here. I was going to lock them up in the desk."

"But there are only boys here. The clerk

at the key booth said it was a girl we were looking for."

Marielle shook her head. "Not necessarily. We now found out that it's a girl who made the copies, but it's not necessarily one of our girls who took the keys in the first place. But I trust every one of these boys here. How could one of them have done something so devious, especially working with a partner? That takes planning." Marielle swept one arm in the air to encompass all the boys busily keyboarding at the computers and racing their helicopters, none of them having any clue they were now considered suspects.

Russ crossed his arms over his chest. "I don't understand what is happening, but the first thing I can think of is that someone is looking for a file. First on the computers in here, then at my house, and now they're looking at the files on the disks. This doesn't make any sense. It's just a bunch of kids."

"Did you see that movie a while back, where a teenage boy hacked into all sorts of military secrets? Could something like that be happening here?"

He stared at Marielle. "Be realistic. That was fiction. Look at your group. Most of them don't have computers at home — they barely know the basics. Not one of them is capable of even a fraction of what you saw in that movie."

Marielle looked up at the clock. "Five minutes, everyone," she called out over her shoulder, "then it's time to go home."

A united groan echoed through the room. But with only a gentle reminder when the clock hit the top of the hour, everyone said goodbye and headed home.

Marielle started at one end of the two tables, Russ at the other, and they met in the middle, shutting all the computers off.

Russ pulled his cell phone off his belt clip. "I just have one more thing to do, now that everyone is gone except you and me." He dragged a chair around the room to all the windows, where he carefully checked for disturbances in the dust patterns. One window appeared to be cleaner than the others, so he took a photo of it with his cell phone.

"This isn't as good as my real camera," he mumbled, "but it will do."

He turned around and hopped off the chair. "I'll compare these at home and see if maybe someone is coming through this window. That may be our answer, although it doesn't look like enough disturbance for a person to have sneaked in."

"Uh, that may have been me. I opened

that window on Friday for a few minutes because it was getting stuffy in here with so many people in the room. These basement windows aren't very big."

The moment of triumph sunk into a puddle at Russ's feet. "Oh well. I tried. Let's go."

As he did every time he gave Marielle a ride, he helped her up into the passenger seat of his SUV, then jogged around to the driver's side.

"I've never had anyone open the door for me like that, yet you've done it before. That seems so old-fashioned."

"My mother taught me manners. I also got very used to opening the door because she had to help support my sister a lot. Sasha spent a lot of time either on crutches or in a wheelchair, and she needed help. We didn't have a car with fancy wheelchair access. I just got the cheapest car I could get that would run, and we made do."

"Oh. I'm so sorry."

"It's okay. We survived."

They were at Marielle's town house much too soon.

He stopped outside of her carport but didn't get out. Instead of looking at Marielle, he looked first at her town house, which was simple and modest, just like Marielle.

He then looked down the block, in the direction of a small playground. Her neighborhood wasn't new, but was well maintained, respectable and practical. Again, just like Marielle.

"How would you like to go to the park or something? Or just take a walk, and then catch dinner somewhere?"

"I'm sorry, I just can't. I have a bunch of stuff I have to do that I've been putting off all week. I should have done it yesterday, but I spent most of yesterday with you." She opened the door and slid out. "Don't worry about seeing me to the door. I'm just going to get in my car, go to the store for a few things and come right back home. I'll see you tomorrow, I guess."

Russ watched her do exactly as she said. He followed her for a few blocks, but didn't go after her when she turned into the parking lot for the grocery store.

The whole way home, all he could think of was Marielle and how in some ways, since he'd met her, his life was so different. For the first time since he could remember, he felt content. Even his ulcer had been acting up less. Yet sometimes he felt his life was spiraling out of his control, and other times he felt like his life had been put on pause and it was time to hit the play button and take back control of the game.

He'd just pulled into his driveway when the musical tone of his cell phone sang out.

He checked the display. "Hey, Marielle. What's up?"

Marielle's voice came out shaky. "I just got home. There was . . . someone in here. I'm so scared."

Russ's heart turned cold. "Get out. Quickly. Don't stay inside. Go to the front and stand under the streetlight and call the police from there. I'll be over as fast as I can."

CHAPTER THIRTEEN

Marielle grabbed her purse and ran out the door. She didn't know why she didn't call the police first. She should have. She would have any other time.

She certainly hadn't called a friend or relative when Russ landed on the roof of her car. She'd automatically dialed 911. Why she had dialed Russ first this time made no sense, but she'd done it.

She'd barely finished giving the dispatcher all the details when Russ's SUV roared into her driveway.

It had barely come to a stop before he got out and barreled toward her.

"What happened? Are you okay?"

"I'm fine, just feeling kind of shaky. When I got home the door wasn't locked. When I went in, just like at your place, everything was fine. My stereo, my DVD player, my computer, everything was still there. But when I started to unpack my groceries I heard the front door squeak and then shut. Someone was in there while I was."

It hadn't hit her before. She'd managed to say the same thing to the police, but in telling Russ, her knees started to tremble, and a chill enveloped her. She refused to cry. But she couldn't stop shaking.

Before she could think, Russ pulled her to him and held her tight. She started to shiver, anyway, but immediately felt warmer, and safe.

"It's okay," he whispered in her ear. "You're fine, and that's all that matters."

A police car with lights flashing but no sirens pulled into her driveway behind Russ's SUV. He let her go when the squad car's door opened and a uniformed officer stepped out.

"Are you Marielle McGee, the occupant?" She nodded.

"Stay here until I come for you." The officer pulled out his gun, and crept into Marielle's town home, poised and ready.

She shuddered. "That gun scares me more than anything."

Neither Russ nor Marielle said a word until the officer returned.

"The intruder is gone. It's safe inside," he said.

Marielle followed the officer, and Russ

trailed her. When they got into the kitchen, Marielle held her purse above the table, ready to put it down between the half-unpacked groceries.

"Can you tell if anything is missing?" the officer asked as he began dusting for finger-prints.

"My purse doesn't feel right." Quickly, she set it down and looked inside. "My wallet is missing!"

A wave of fear surged through her, even though she was certainly safe with both Russ and a police officer here.

She looked up into the officer's warm brown eyes. "I can't believe this. I had a couple of bags of groceries when I walked in, and I thought I was going to drop something, so I put my purse down on the floor in the hallway and went into the kitchen." Her knees started to shake, and mechanically, she walked to the door. "While I was in the kitchen, there was someone here, going through my purse!" She turned to the officer, who had followed her. "What am I going to do?"

"Cancel your credit cards right now, and you'll have to get duplicates made of your driver's license and other identification. Identity theft has become a major problem. You'll still have to watch your personal accounts for a long time after you get your new cards."

She sagged and looked at the floor where her purse had been. Suddenly, it hit her. "My keys are missing, too. I left them on the floor beside my purse when I came in!"

She ran to the window to make sure her car was still in the carport. "I have a spare key, but if someone else does, too, and they know where I live, my car isn't safe. I'll have to get a locksmith to change the locks tonight." She buried her face in her hands. "I can't afford a weekend callout. I don't even have my credit cards to pay for this."

Russ stepped beside her. "Let me pay for that. I certainly owe you more. I insist."

"Excuse me." The officer cleared his throat. "Can I ask you a few questions to fill out my report? And then I'll be on my way."

Marielle nodded weakly. "Certainly." Numbly, she answered all the officer's queries.

When he left, Russ stayed with her.

"I want to take all my registration and stuff out of the glovebox, just in case," she said.

She stepped outside and into the driveway, and again, Russ followed her. She was almost done removing everything out of the glovebox when he appeared beside the car door.

"Marielle, what color is your wallet?"

"It's brown. Why?"

"Is this it?" He held up a wallet.

Her wallet.

Marielle gasped. "Yes!"

She nearly grabbed it out of his hands. "Everything is in here except for the cash! And there wasn't much money anyway." She sprang out of the car and threw her arms around Russ's neck.

His arms wrapped around her waist, but instead of dancing like she was doing, he stayed very still. When she stilled, he lowered his head and rested his cheek on the top of her head.

He didn't say a word. He just held her.

A million reasons why she shouldn't have been enjoying the warm fuzzies passed through her head. But she couldn't help it. She hugged him back.

She'd seldom had anyone to just hold her, except maybe her mother when she was a child. But really, neither of her parents were huggy types. Michael had never held her just to offer comfort. In fact, the closer they got to the day that was supposed to be their wedding, the more Michael's hands had roamed — to the point that she often felt uncomfortable.

She'd never felt uncomfortable with Russ. By nature, he seemed gentle and controlled, but today she'd seen another side of him. The expression on his face when he came to her aid today told her how he cared about her. For a man who spent most of his day sitting behind a desk, he had moved fast.

She'd been in love before, but what she felt now was different. Michael had hurt her so badly she'd barely survived, and in hindsight, she could see that Michael had had it in him all along to be totally self-centered.

Russ wasn't cold and calculated in his pursuit of what he wanted, like Michael was. But, like Michael, Russ still had considerable drive. It was different, but he was also driven. She hadn't quite figured it out, but figuring it out didn't change it or protect her from being hurt by it. Russ was on his way up the corporate ladder, and he was very honest and up-front about it. He lived in his own self-sufficient world, and his foray into helping the teens, no matter how much good he was doing, and no matter how much they liked him, didn't change anything.

He was going to leave, and he wouldn't look back.

She wanted to kiss him now, because she was positive that he would kiss her back.

Except she'd lost at love before.

She didn't want to lose again.

So Marielle raised her palms to his chest and pushed very gently, knowing that he would respect her wishes and back away.

Which, of course, he did.

"I should get back in the house. The reason I wanted to come straight home is that I had so much to do. Now I've lost even more time."

She turned around and stepped toward the door, but a flash of silver made her stop in her tracks.

"My keys!"

"Are you sure?"

"Yes. See my pink pompom?"

She picked them up, but they didn't feel right. She weighed it in her hand, then inspected each key.

"Some are missing. My house key is here, so is my car key." She mentally counted them off. "This is so strange. The ones missing are for things no one could get any access to. The filing cabinet at the office, the shed in my complex where they pile up the newspapers until the recycling truck comes, the lock to my friend's camper."

"What about the key to the church basement?"

"Too much weight on a key chain is bad for your ignition switch, so I have a separate key chain for the church keys because I have so many. The front door, the basement, the storage locker, the desk, and the closet for the cleaning supplies. That key chain is still in my pocket."

"So the only keys that are missing are for odd, unrelated things?"

"Yes." Marielle lowered her hands to her sides. "This doesn't make any sense."

"A lot of things aren't making any sense. But there has to be a connection. When I go to the center tomorrow I'll talk to Pastor Tom and see if anyone else has had similar problems. At least you know there wasn't enough time for anyone to have copied any of your keys."

"I don't know why anyone would want to get into the recycling shed. I'm not even going to bother reporting that to the strata committee. People lose their keys for that all the time. They don't even care. I don't know why it's locked in the first place."

"I would think to keep out the vagrants. It's a shelter in the cold weather."

"You're probably right."

"But I do know one thing. Your intruder

was a woman."

"How do you know that? Did you see someone?"

"No, but I smelled some kind of perfume residue. The thing is, I've smelled it before and I can't remember where. I just know that I've never smelled it on you. So it was a woman who was here, and we know it's a woman who helped herself to my keys. I don't believe in coincidences."

"You could be right. Someone seems to be targeting our church people."

"Maybe. I always talk to Pastor Tom before he lets me in every day. I'll run it by him, and I'll let you know what he says."

CHAPTER FOURTEEN

Russ tried to be discreet as he studied his half of the teen group. Was anyone overly nervous? Was anyone too interested in anything not directly related to them?

He couldn't see anything amiss, and it bothered him.

Maybe there was nothing wrong. Maybe he was imagining connections, and in fact everything that had happened was random and unrelated.

It was almost time to go, and he'd found nothing — neither had Marielle. Pastor Tom was concerned, of course, but he didn't have any ideas or suggestions, other than to be careful, and to be doubly sure everything was securely locked up when they left.

"Russ?" said Jason. "Can you come here? I found a file in a strange place. I don't know what to do."

"What's up?"

Russ leaned over Jason's shoulder while

the teen highlighted a file. "I changed the settings to show hidden files so I can clean out my temp files, and I found this. It's not mine. I don't want to delete it until I'm sure you don't need it."

"It's okay. You've got the computer that used to be mine. I copied everything I needed, so I wouldn't have to reinstall the operating system. Anything that's not an executable file can be . . ." He let his voice trail off when he read the file name. "Wait. You're right. Don't delete that one. That's the name of one of my biggest clients, but I would never put a file like that in a hidden directory. Why is this here?"

Jason slid off the chair for Russ to take his place. Russ pulled a flash drive out of his pocket and plugged it into the USB port. "I don't remember this file, so I think I'll copy it and take it home to see what it is." As he dragged the file to copy it, he couldn't believe the size of it. "There, it's done. Now finish up what you're doing — it's almost time to go home."

He helped Marielle lock up, making sure the doors were locked and the windows secured. He waved as she drove off, then he unlocked his security bar and tucked it under the car seat.

This time, Russ didn't stop to pick up a

coffee and he changed his original plans for a side trip to the grocery store for milk. Today, he went straight home and headed for the computer in his den.

Nothing he tried could open the mystery file, so he left-clicked on the name, which gave him the time the file was last updated.

He stared at the date and time. It wasn't right. The file showed the last update was the day before his accident, but the last time he'd worked on it was on the weekend, at home. He hadn't done anything to it at the office for at least a week because he'd been too busy with other things.

But he knew who had.

Jessie.

Russ hit the autodial on his cell phone and waited for Marielle to answer.

He leaned back in the chair and rested one arm on top of his head as he spoke. "Jason found the strangest thing on my old computer at the center. I brought the file home, and it appears to be something that Jessie and I were working on, except the date is wrong and I can't open the file."

"I really doubt there's anything I can help you with," she said.

"I didn't want to talk to you about the computer. I wanted to talk to you about Jessie."

"Your co-worker."

He leaned back in the chair. "Yes. I was talking to Grant, and it was Jessie who was up there and stuck her head out the window after I fell. Grant says she wasn't with the office crowd, but he wouldn't know if she was just standing around anywhere else. Do you know if she was?"

"I don't think so, but I'm not sure."

"She's about five foot six inches, she's got dark brown hair, shoulder length. No curl — it just kind of hangs there. I can't remember what she was wearing, but she always wears pants, never a skirt, and she wears these punk-style boots all the time."

"No. I didn't see anyone like that outside. But Russ, I *was* a bit distracted."

Russ thought back to that day. He remembered talking to Jessie when she first arrived at the office. He remembered walking with her into his office and sitting down at his computer as he was trying to install a new program that wasn't going very well.

The image of getting up and walking to the window formed in his mind as if he were looking through fog, then went blank.

"Russ? Are you there?"

He pressed his fingers to the bridge of his nose. "Yes. I think I just remembered something. I actually recall walking to the window that day. But I don't know why. And I think I remember Jessie being in my office at the time. It's still not clear, and when I try to remember, it fades away."

"That's a start, so that's good. Have you talked to Jessie about it?"

"No. Every time I try to call I only get her voice mail, and the last time I called, her voice-mail box was full."

"Do you know where she lives? Can you go to her home?"

"I don't have that. But that's a good idea. Grant has to have some kind of address on her, I would think. She's a contract employee, not a regular staff person. She makes her own hours, depending on the project."

"So what is Jessie's connection to the file?"

"Like I said, the file is in a hidden directory and it's been masked, yet it's clearly named for the last file I was working on with Jessie. But strangely, it was last updated after the date I last worked on it. That tells me that something's wrong, but I'm not sure what. I guess I'm using you as a sounding board to help me think out loud. I hope you don't mind."

"Of course I don't mind. I want to help."

"This is really bothering me. I've made some progress and got it to open, but it's been encrypted in such a way that I can't view it properly. I can tell from the extension that it's probably a video file of some kind. There wasn't any video in the project, so I have no idea what this is, or why it was in an obscure directory. It's like I was trying to hide it — except it's not my file, even though it was on my computer."

"If you were working on the project together, maybe Jessie was doing some work on your computer and forgot to tell you."

He shook his head even though Marielle wasn't there to see him. "That's not possible. She always brings her laptop. I'm at the office more than Jessie. If she did anything on my computer, I couldn't do anything but stand there and watch her. I don't have anyplace to work except for my own desk."

"Russ, I just heard a beep, my battery is dying. If you need someone to talk to, I can come over there. Or maybe if you try to show me the file, working on it might trigger some kind of memory for you."

"You don't have to do that."

"But I want to. I can't imagine what it must be like to not be able to remember something so important. This is also affecting me."

He stared at his computer. She was right. Talking out loud about it had already helped him remember something that was impor-tant. "Have you had supper yet? I can cook something. It's the least I can do if you're going to come all this way."

"That would be gr —" The line went dead.

Russ hadn't heard what she was going to say, but he'd heard enough to know that she was coming.

He left the computer and went into the kitchen to see what he could scrounge together to feed two people on short notice. Waiting for a package of ground beef to defrost gave him more time to think.

He couldn't imagine why he would have gone to the window that day when he was busy. Also, being busy, he wouldn't have let Jessie work on his computer and tie it up. Yet if one of Jessie's files was on his com-puter, was the work something she couldn't do on her laptop?

He couldn't *remember.* Just trying to remember made everything sink deeper into the fog.

But even if there was something she needed to do on his computer that day, that didn't explain the date of the file — the Friday before his accident. He'd had an emergency come up for another client, so he hadn't worked on it that day. The last time he'd worked on it was the day before

— Thursday.

Unless he'd let Jessie use his computer then, too. Except he knew he hadn't. He could remember everything from that Friday because he'd been in panic mode over a project shutdown.

He had the ground beef fried and was ready to add a can of spaghetti sauce, when the doorbell rang. He opened the door to Marielle, exactly as he'd left her, except her hair was messier. He didn't want to stare, but he couldn't help it. While Marielle never dressed up, her hair was always neatly combed. The difference made him want to reach out and make it as neat as it always was, but not with a comb — with his fingers — slowly, and gently. And while he was doing that, he would naturally hold her, make the moment last. Maybe even spend extra time playing with that silly red stripe in her hair.

But he didn't have that right. It hit him squarely in the gut how much he wanted her to be with him, even though the supper he was making was certainly nothing special.

She smiled at him. "Hey."

"Hey, back. I hope you don't mind spaghetti."

"I love spaghetti."

The favorite meal of a single man, he

thought. And apparently a single woman, too.

She followed him into the kitchen. As he continued to cook, Marielle opened a few cupboard doors until she found the plates, and began setting the table.

"I was thinking on the way here. The more you tell me, the less I can figure out what you were doing at the window when you were busy."

He nodded. "I know. I also don't understand how I could have fallen. It's not like I was doing something stupid or risky. How exactly would anyone fall through a window? The only explanation would be if I was climbing out for some reason, and slipped — or if I was pushed. Neither one makes sense."

"I agree. Why would you have been on the ledge?"

"I wouldn't. It's too risky, and I don't take risks — at least not that kind. That ledge out there is barely wide enough for the pigeons, never mind my size twelves."

The table set, she turned around and put her hands on her hips. "You wear size twelve shoes?"

He stirred the sauce vigorously. "I'm six feet tall. I should have a shoe size to match, don't you think?" He grinned.

Marielle continued in a serious vein. "But the only other possibility is that you were pushed. And that would be . . ."

". . . attempted murder."

Russ and Marielle stared at each other.

"That would certainly explain why Jessie seems to have disappeared."

"But Jessie isn't a bad person. I've worked with her off and on for about a year. She wouldn't hurt a fly."

"Even mafia murderers are good people to their mothers. And whenever you read in the paper that someone committed murder and only a thorough investigation uncovers it, usually the neighbors say what a nice person they were."

"But Jessie . . ." Russ let his voice trail off as he thought about Jessie. It wasn't possible that she had it in her to try to kill someone, least of all him. But then, he didn't have it in him to do something stupid like climb outside a window and stand on a ledge barely big enough for his toes. The only other possibility was that he was leaning out the window too far and fell.

"I plan to speak with Jessie, but I've also got to find out what was on that file. I think that's where I'm going to find the answers I need."

"Did you say that Jason found it in the

first place?"

"Yes. It was by accident, but he was sharp enough to know not to delete it. He's got a lot of potential."

"Yes. I'm positive he's going to be able to get out of that neighborhood and live a decent, normal life." Marielle's voice dropped to barely above a whisper. "Just like you."

The reminder stabbed him like a knife. That was exactly why he didn't want to be part of that group. It brought to mind what he'd escaped and how hard he'd had to work to do it, along with the personal scars he'd had to endure. He wanted to put those days behind him, and keep them behind him.

Jason also deserved to have everything put behind him. So did everyone in that youth group.

But statistically, only a small portion of the group would be able to get out. Most of them were doomed to repeat the lives of their parents.

"For you have the poor with you always . . ." Mark 14:7

It wasn't fair, but then, life wasn't always fair. Everyone had to make choices, and the result in a person's life would depend on the choices he made, and how he handled the harder ones.

Like whether Russ should stick with the church group, or, when his required time was up, shake the dust off his sandals and move on.

For the first time, he didn't know what to do.

"I think the spaghetti is cooked. Let's eat," he said.

Marielle sat while he served, then Russ sat and folded his hands in front of him, bowed his head.

"Dear Lord, thank You for this food and this day. Thank You also for the freedom You give us to make the choices You give us . . . including the freedom to make the wrong choices."

He had to trust that God would guide him to make the decision that was best in the end. Just like Russ had made the decision with his sister. Everything had worked out in the end. God had been faithful in the things that were important, despite how hard Russ's life had been. His sister was okay, and his mother was happily remarried. God had told him what to do, and Russ had trusted God and followed.

It was just that for all the ten years it took, Russ hadn't been able to see that it had been part of the bigger plan. He'd held it all against God — the hard work, the long hours. But now, after so many surgeries, his sister was happy and a productive member of society, and his mother was free of all the accumulated debts — the medical expenses and the bills his father had left them with. Finally Russ could see things more clearly. His family's needs had made him a more responsible person, and now, finally, he was responsible only for himself.

He didn't want to get involved in something else that would tie him down again.

"Amen," he said.

"Amen," Marielle answered, and immediately started eating, which told Russ how hungry she was.

"This sauce is great. You're a good cook," she said.

Russ toyed with a length of spaghetti on his fork. "Not really. It's just the canned stuff with a bit of extra oregano."

"My fiancé was a good cook, too."

Suddenly, Russ was no longer hungry. "Fiancé?"

"Yes. I was engaged once. Didn't Pastor Tom tell you?"

"No, he didn't."

She sighed. "Michael dumped me a couple of days before what was supposed to be our wedding. If I have to look back and see something good, at least he didn't leave me at the altar."

"Do you want to talk about it? It's okay if you don't."

"I'm sure you're curious." She sighed and continued. "He was a real go-getter, moving up early in the corporate world. Just like you. He worked, and I worked to help support him — even to the detriment of my own college education. But in the end, everything that I thought we were doing for 'us,' was really all just for him." She laughed dryly. "In the end, he found my lack of higher education and corporate sophistication unworthy of a man like himself. So he dumped me for another woman."

"You make it sound so cut-and-dried. Things are seldom that simple."

"But sometimes they are. He married someone who was just as ambitious as himself. They have a huge house, three cars between the two of them, a foo-foo dog with a fussy haircut, a live-in housekeeper and no children. They say they're happy, but I don't know if they know how to be happy — they're too busy working for the next 'best' of whatever is the latest trend."

"That sounds so shallow."

"It's not a sin to be rich. People get it wrong all the time. It's not that money is the root of all evil. It's the *love* of money that's the bad thing."

"You sound like you're making excuses for him." He stiffened and sucked in a deep breath. "Do you still love him?"

"No. I can say that without a doubt. It wouldn't have worked between us, I can see that, but it sure hurt at the time."

"I'm so sorry, but glad you're here now."

"And I'm glad *you're* here. Now let's go see if you can show me anything with that file."

Russ led her down the hall to the den, but as he walked he kept hearing her words in his mind.

Just like you.

Was he really as selfish as this other guy? Russ knew he worked a lot of hours, including weekends. That wasn't so bad. Lots of people did it. He didn't know why it was somehow okay to work two jobs and do nothing but work and sleep if a person was completely broke, but *not* okay if a person worked extra hard, even had two jobs, if he was well-off.

"It's not a sin to work hard, either, you know," he blurted out. "That's the only way that poor people can get ahead. Is there some line where you have to stop working hard once you pass a certain level?"

"You make it sound like I'm accusing you of something, and I'm not."

"Maybe not, but you've hit a nerve."

"I didn't mean to. I'm sorry. Now let's see what you can do with that file."

Grateful for the change in subject, Russ opened the directory. "This file has to be the reason for all our troubles. Think about it. It was on the computer that used to be mine at the office. That's the same computer that was left on at the center. No one can get in without the password, so whoever was trying to find this file wasn't successful. That would also explain why they went to my home computer and nowhere else in the house. They must have been hoping I would have a copy on my hard drive here."

"Why would they go to *my* house, then? I wouldn't be taking home copies of your files."

"No, but they didn't go after your computer. The thing that went missing was keys."

"Keys for non-related things."

"Maybe, maybe not. I was thinking, this all points to Jessie. This is a project we were working on together. She doesn't know the password to get into this computer, so after not finding the file on my home computer, the next step would be to try to try to figure out the password. But if time is limited, if she couldn't take the time here, then the way to have more time would be to take the computer and try someplace else. But we've got the computers all locked down. I don't have keys on my chain, but for all she knew, maybe you did, because you're the leader there. I think she was looking for the key for the computer so she could steal it and take it home to figure out my password."

"So what do we do?"

"I have to know why she wants this file so bad."

"I don't understand how it could be on your computer in the first place, if you're password protected."

"Jessie is in and out of our office all the time. I don't lock up my computer when I'm gone for breaks — there's no reason to. The office isn't open to the public, it's only other staff. It would have been easy for Jessie to have transferred this file onto my computer when I was away on a break. I just don't understand why."

"You say she was in your office the day of the accident. Why didn't she just transfer it off then, while you were out cold lying on my car."

"Because I had just started a reboot, and Jessie doesn't have the password. Hey. I just remembered something. It just came naturally. That feels so good."

"What happened after you rebooted?"

"I don't remember finishing. I just remember getting really frustrated with a new program installation, and then having to reboot twice."

Marielle went silent, and Russ assumed that she was going to let him try to remember what happened. He closed his eyes and pressed his fingertips to his temples.

"Nothing else is coming. I remember feeling the frustration, and I remember standing up and turning to the window. That's all. But at least I'm not getting a headache anymore when I try to think about it."

"Then maybe you shouldn't overdo it."

Russ drew in a deep breath and sighed. "Of course you're right. Now that we know what's happening, I should be concentrating on catching her in the act."

Marielle held up her palm. "Not so fast. What if we're putting two and two together, and coming up with five?"

Russ frowned. "You're right. It makes sense to us, but really, we don't have any solid proof. We have to catch whoever is doing this actually doing something before we go making accusations, or alarming Pastor Tom."

Marielle pointed to the door leading to the hall. "If it is Jessie, she's either got a key or she's coming in through a window somewhere and then just walking through the halls and going wherever she wants."

"I know. I've looked at the locks. The outside door locks are dead bolts, but everything else in the building is old and not made for security. All the inside doors, including the one to the youth center room, can be opened with a credit card. I just haven't done it because I didn't want to insult Pastor Tom."

Marielle grinned. "I know. I've done that a couple of times, when I accidentally left my keys in the room and didn't feel like going outside the building and all the way around to the other door."

Russ grinned. "That's pretty funny. I hope you didn't get caught."

Marielle grinned back. "I hope not. I could get fired for being a bad example." Her grin dropped. "I just thought of something. Your keys and the disks disappeared when we were both here. That means she has to have a helper. There have been a lot of people here lately that I've never seen before. If this file is important enough for Jessie to go to all this trouble, it's got to be very important. Do you think she might have pushed you, and it's the shock that's making you unable to remember?"

"I hope not." But Russ had already thought the same thing. What worried him more than anything was that if Jessie had deliberately pushed him out the window and nearly killed him, then she would be equally capable of doing the same to Marielle.

The possibility terrified him.

Which made it even more imperative that he get into the file as quickly as he could.

He turned around, not looking at Marielle as he spoke. "But just the same, just in case she has gone off the deep end, I want you to promise me that you'll be really careful, and that you won't go into places where you'll be vulnerable and alone." Marielle was the most predictable person he'd ever met; he could time her entrances and her exits with a stopwatch every day. And though it was one of the things that made her so charming, it also put her at risk of being tailed.

"I think it's time I went home, it's getting late," she said.

Russ wanted to ask if he could follow her home, just to be sure she was safe, but he had a feeling he knew what kind of reaction he would get.

"Before you go, I want to give you something." He reached into his pocket. "I'm not really comfortable with this, but I don't know what else to do. I want you to take my flash drive, and as soon as you get home, hide it somewhere safe, where no one but you will find it. Don't keep it in your purse or anywhere on you. The file is copied onto it. If something happens to me, I want you to turn this over to the police."

Her face paled.

"Don't worry. Now that I'm starting to think we might have figured something out, I know to be extra careful. I hate doing this to you, but a backup is only as good as the storage, and storage is safest at a remote location. I don't know who else I can trust until I get this mess sorted out. I don't even like it being in your purse for the amount of time it's going to take you to get home, but I don't think we have a choice. You don't have to stop anywhere tonight, do you?"

"No. I'm going straight home. I can think of a few places already that no one would find it. I'll see you tomorrow. I sure hope you can find out what that file is and why it's so important to her."

CHAPTER FIFTEEN

"I'm glad we're both here early today. I found one of the windows unlocked when I got here. I know we double-checked them all on Sunday. What do you think of that?"

Marielle turned and stared at the closest window. A cold shiver of dread tingled up her spine. "Maybe it was just someone coming in for a warm, dry place to spend the night. It's a church, after all."

"Do you really believe that?"

Marielle tried not to let the nervousness show through in her voice. "No. Not really."

"I didn't think so. I don't think that, either. What I do think is that something is rotten in the state of Denmark."

"Where did that expression come from?"

"Shakespeare. *Hamlet.*"

"What have you been doing here all this time? Surely not just walking around checking doors and windows."

"I've been trying to get this file to open,

and I'm more than a little frustrated. I've uninstalled and reinstalled different versions of several programs more times than I can count. Nothing seems to work. I can't figure out her encryption."

"Are you saying that you won't be able to open the file?"

"I have a few more things to try, but it doesn't look good."

One thing that did look good to her, though, was Russ, stretched out as casually as could be on the chair.

The way he was sprawled out emphasized his trim waistline and the length of his legs. Despite the heavy topic of conversation, the casual position made him look playful, and the little bump on his nose hinted at a bad-boy attitude, whether he had it or not. He probably didn't realize that he'd mussed his hair, making him look just untidy enough that it begged her to run her fingers through his hair.

He was smart, and he was good-looking.

"Sit up straight," she grumbled, trying to control her errant thoughts. "That's bad for your posture."

He also was good at following instructions, because he immediately sat straight and planted both feet flat on the floor, setting his legs at forty-five-degree angles. He positioned himself with his back perfectly straight, and his hands slightly over elbow height at the keyboard.

"You must type a lot, don't you."

He nodded as he punched in a few keys, then hit enter and waited to see what would happen. "Yup. Last time I took a typing test I clocked myself at seventy-five words per minute. But I know I could do better now."

He was a good typist, too.

More and more, she wanted to find some fatal flaw about him. Something that would make her *not* like him.

"I plan on being early every day this week. I want to surprise our unwelcome guest and catch her red-handed trying to hack into this computer."

"What about next week, when you're not here? What will happen then?"

His hands stilled over the keyboard. "I'm going to do everything in my power to get this thing settled this week. I'm going to find out what's in this file if it kills me. When I know what this is, then I'll know how to deal with Jessie."

Marielle pressed her fingers to her temples. "Has Grant managed to get a hold of her yet?"

"Nope. That would make things easier, but no one has heard from her."

Marielle turned her head toward the desk. "I should check that pile of disks to make sure nothing's been added or deleted."

"Good idea."

Marielle checked the disks one at a time. To make the task less tedious, she watched Russ at work as he continued in his attempts to gain access to the file. She'd never seen such concentration. Nothing distracted him. Even though he'd admitted to being frustrated, he seemed the epitome of patience as he tried and tried again. Still, nothing worked.

When her last disk was checked and the contents confirmed unchanged, Marielle sat back and waited for the youth group to arrive.

Everything proceeded normally that day, except when it came time to let everyone practice what they had learned. Today, instead of standing and watching, Russ returned to his own computer, and his mission.

Jason seemed mesmerized watching Russ in action. After only a few minutes, he abandoned his computer and stood beside Russ for a while as Russ continued his efforts. Marielle watched from her desk as Jason dragged a chair and sat beside Russ, and the two of them talked while Russ worked.

She couldn't hear what they were saying, but when Jason said something, then pointed to one of the files in a window Russ had opened, Russ stiffened, then began frantically keying in, hit enter, and sat back.

A video began to take shape on the monitor.

Marielle stood and pushed her chair away so fast she nearly sent it crashing to the floor. She ran across the room to see a video of a man and a woman, who didn't look like they knew they were being filmed, walking through a mall, holding hands. The man carried a number of bags that appeared to be from an upscale ladies boutique.

"I know this man," Russ said. "He's currently our biggest client. It's really strange, but a few days before my accident, he told me he wanted to push everything ahead, and then after, Grant told me he had put everything on hold. I wish I knew why Jessie has this video, and why she's gone to such lengths to recover it."

The camera zoomed in closer, and Russ knew. "That woman isn't his wife."

The man in the video leaned down and brushed a kiss onto the woman's cheek. She turned her head, they exchanged a short kiss, and then they kept walking.

Russ put the video on pause. "I can't watch this."

Marielle's stomach tightened into a painful knot. She didn't know this man, or his wife, but her heart ached for the woman, and she tried not to hate the man or the woman he was with.

She couldn't help but be reminded of her fiancé. When Michael had said he didn't want to marry her, that had been enough of a shock. Her first question had been whether there was another woman, and Michael had said there wasn't. She'd believed him, but then, when she was in the middle of the heart-wrenching process of canceling all their wedding plans, she had discovered there *was* another woman. And worse, many of the guests who would have been at their wedding had *known* about the other woman. She couldn't believe that her so-called friends — friends that she had invited to her wedding — hadn't told her.

Russ made a few adjustments to enlarge the picture. "There's something wrong here."

"Of course there's something wrong!" Marielle snapped. "The man is cheating on his wife!"

"No. Not that. It's the resolution." He backed up a few frames and stopped at the point when they were separating after their kiss.

Marielle couldn't look. The situation brought back all the heartache of Michael's betrayal and his criticism of her shortcomings, which he explained in detail one by one. He had even said that everything that happened, including his finding another woman, was Marielle's fault. He had told her Elaine was everything that Marielle wasn't.

She closed her eyes, trying to calm the turmoil inside her, but curiosity got the better of her and she opened them again.

Russ had enlarged the picture even more, until just the faces filled the screen.

Marielle knew she was on the verge of tears. She gritted her teeth and forced herself to take short shallow breaths to control herself.

"There. Jason, Marielle, look at this." Being careful not to touch the monitor with his fingers, Russ picked up a pen and pointed to a few spots in the image. "See? Right here. This isn't right. This has been digitally altered." He backed up a few more frames, enlarged them, and then pointed to the same area in the previous frame. "See how it's different? They should be the same. In real time, those frames would have been less than a second apart."

Jason nodded. "Yes, I can see it now." He turned to Russ. "So this means that the images of this guy have been added over top of someone else?"

"Exactly."

"I don't understand," Marielle said.

Russ turned to her. "It means that this situation really didn't happen. This woman was kissing someone, but it wasn't Byron. He's been added to the video. The images of his face have been planted frame by frame over top of those of the man that this really happened to."

"I still don't understand. For what purpose?"

"I'm not sure I do, either. Doing something like this is a lot of work. Every frame has to be worked at pixel by pixel in the area to be changed. What we've seen so far would have taken months to do. It's done really well, too. I wouldn't have noticed if I hadn't put it on pause — and I'm an expert at this kind of thing."

"What does this mean?"

Russ stared at the screen. "The only reason I can think of to make a video like this would be to try to blackmail someone. Why would Jessie want to make someone think Byron was having an affair? Who would she show this video to?"

"Or maybe it's the other way around," Jason said. "Maybe she made it *not* to be shown. Or to be shown only once. To this guy in the picture."

Russ's eyes widened. "That explains it. The way Byron ended the project so abruptly, it looked like he suddenly ran out of money. I wonder if Jessie showed this to him, and then threatened to show his wife. She could be using this for extortion."

"But you just said it's a fake."

He turned to her. "Sometimes that doesn't matter. First, Byron would have to *prove* it's fake, but in the time it would take to get the evidence, the damage would already be done. His wife would feel the betrayal. Even finding out the video was fake, that sense of betrayal could never be completely erased. She'd never be completely sure, and she might never trust him again. That's why lawyers say things to the jury they know they're not supposed to say, and then retract it. They're planting seeds to make their case, knowing that once said, right or wrong, the words can't be erased from a person's memory."

"Yeah," Jason said. "It's like when some-one says something really mean to you, then laughs and says they're just kidding. But it still hurts because it's already been said."

All the things Michael had said when he told her he couldn't marry her roared through her head — that she wasn't good enough for a man who had ambition, that she wasn't smart enough because she didn't go to college. But it wasn't that she didn't *want* to go to college. It was that she'd been working two jobs to pay tuition for Michael to go to college. Plus she often helped him with his research. By the time he graduated, she was burned out, and told him she wanted some downtime to prepare for her own college adventure. Instead of respecting her needs, or being thankful that she'd nearly driven herself to the point of exhaustion for him, he'd called her lazy and unmotivated, then had accused her of planning to sit back and do nothing after they were married. Of course that wasn't true, but Michael wouldn't listen as she tried to defend herself. Nothing she said could change his mind. He'd gone on to say that no one would ever love someone like her because she was unwilling to better herself.

He'd even said that the reason he'd found someone else was that Marielle was never around when he needed her, and when she was around, too often she fell asleep on the couch, proving that she was indeed lazy.

She would never forget Michael's hurtful words for as long as she lived. For a long time, she'd believed they were true. It had taken a lot of healing for her to put the hurt behind her.

Her lower lip started to quiver and the backs of her eyes burned. She couldn't stop it.

A tear rolled down her cheek.

"Marielle? Jason, can you excuse us?"

Before Marielle knew what was happening, Russ stood, took hold of her elbow and guided her through the inside door.

He shut the door behind them so they stood alone in the hallway. "What's wrong?" he asked gently.

"I know how that woman is going to feel," she choked out, then began to sob.

Russ wrapped his arms around her and held her tight as she cried uncontrollably into his chest.

When she had cried herself out, Russ ran his fingers through her hair. "Was your ex-fiancé cheating on you?" he asked.

She nodded a few times in rapid succession, keeping her face pressed against his shirt so he wouldn't see her bloodshot eyes or puffy cheeks. "Just like everyone says, I was the last to know. In addition to feeling totally betrayed, I felt so stupid. I know exactly how Byron's wife is going to feel. Even if he does prove later that the video is a fake, the hurt is going to happen."

"I can only guess. I'm so sorry that happened to you." He pressed his cheek to the top of her head. "You're too special to be treated like that."

"You don't have to say things like that when you know they're not true."

"But it *is* true, and don't let anyone ever tell you different. Are you okay now? We've got to get back in there. We've left the teens on their own and they're going to start wondering where we've gone."

Russ returned to the youth center while Marielle ran to the washroom to splash some cold water on her face. By the time she returned to the room, only a few of the teens remained, which was a profound relief.

She kept herself busy until the last few left, then Russ joined her.

"This really changes things. What we saw took months of work. I can see why Jessie is going to such extremes to get it back. I know she only has one computer — her laptop. She backs up her files on our company server, but if this is something she didn't want to put on our server because she didn't want anyone to have access to it, putting it on my computer in a hidden file is the perfect place to hide it. I know her laptop crashed the night before my accident, so that means the copy she had for safekeeping on my computer became the only copy. That would explain why she's going through such efforts to get it."

"What about your client, Byron? If this is the only copy, then he's safe," said Marielle.

"Yes, but he won't know she no longer has it in her possession. She wouldn't threaten extortion, then admit she had lost her dirty work. If I tell Jessie we're on to her, then she should back off. Except, she seems to have disappeared. Grant can't find her, I've left messages on her voice mail. I'd think she had disappeared off the face of the earth, except we know she's been around here."

Marielle frowned and rested her closed fists on her hips. "If she won't go into the office, and you can't reach her at home, then it looks like there's nothing you can do."

"Then I have to find another way to catch her."

"How?"

Russ smiled. "I have something at home. I'll be in early again tomorrow, so I'll set it up when I get here. But in the meantime . . ."

Russ returned to the computer and began keyboarding. "I'm going to leave the file here — two can play at this little game. Now that I've got it open, I'm going to put in my own encryptions, so when Jessie gets it and tries to open it, she won't be able to access it."

Marielle tidied up and double-checked the windows while Russ worked.

"There. I'm done," he said a few minutes later. "Tomorrow, we'll see what happens."

CHAPTER SIXTEEN

The next day Marielle hovered over Russ's chair, but Russ wasn't in it. He was on his hands and knees under the table.

She bent at the waist and looked down. "What are you doing under there?"

Russ backed out, sat and dusted off his knees. Then he set a circular device on the table and tilted it toward her. "Smile," he said, grinning. "You're on *Candid Camera.*"

"Candid Camera?"

"It's a webcam. Tonight, if she comes, I'll have this pointed toward my computer and I can watch remotely from home."

"You don't think you're going to be up all night, and then still come here during the daytime?"

"Oops. I never thought of that. Wait, I have an idea. It's just an Internet link. I'll set it up so you can watch from your home on your home computer, too. We can take turns watching. Would that work for you?"

"Only if I can still go to bed on time. I have to get up early, you know."

"At this point, any little bit would help. Without telling Grant what I found, I asked him for Jessie's address. She wasn't there, and according to her neighbors, she hasn't been home for weeks. They thought she was on vacation, so I didn't enlighten them. We're going to have to catch her here, with this." He patted the top of the webcam.

"What happens when we *do* catch her?"

"As soon as I type in a message, the screen over there will light up, it will make a little noise, and then Jessie will read what I've got on there. It'll be a note advising her to stop what she's doing and tell Byron she's going to leave him alone. Also, when she comes in, we can call the police and they can arrest her for B and E. But even if the police don't make it in time to catch her inside the building, the video will be a permanent record of what she's done. It wouldn't be admissible in court, but we could use the video to bring Jessie out in the open."

"Do you think that's going to work?"

"I can't see why not."

"Okay, then let's see what happens. You'd better put it away for now. The kids are going to start arriving any minute."

No sooner had she spoken when Jason walked in. Russ quickly unplugged the webcam and tucked it away.

"By the way, I think I found out how she's been getting in here," said Russ.

Marielle checked to make sure Jason was far away enough that he wouldn't hear their conversation, then stepped closer to Russ. "How?"

"I think she's been climbing up the trellis and coming in through the second-floor window, then simply walking down here and using a card or something to jimmy the lock on the inside door. A few days ago I asked Pastor Tom to tell whoever is cleaning not to dust around the windows. I also told him what I think is happening, but not to be alarmed — that this is just between me and Jessie, and I want to stop it. The next time she comes in, we should be able to confirm which window she's using by a clean spot on the ledge."

"Good idea." She scanned the room. "It looks like almost everybody is here. We should start."

A typical afternoon with the teens had never passed so slowly. But finally, Marielle was able to sit in the comfort of her den and watch the youth center from her home computer, via the webcam.

While she kept an eye on the computer, she sorted all her laundry, caught up on her ironing, and even did a little knitting. But soon, she found it frustrating that she was unable to leave the room to do something else, including go to the washroom.

Suddenly, a face flashed across the screen, but not the face of a woman she didn't know. It was Russ. The image moved in jerky patterns, then waved. She could see his den furniture in the background, so she knew he was at his home and not at the church.

A message appeared across the display box.

Russ999: Are you having fun yet?

Marielle typed her own message using the screen name Russ had set up for her.

Merrymari: I'm not sure. I haven't seen anyone yet.

Russ999: She may not come tonight. I thought I'd check up on you and see if you were bored. These chat programs can be a lot of fun, but only if there's someone interesting to talk to.

Marielle smiled.

Merrymari: Then I hope that someone interesting comes real soon.

Russ999: haha very funny

She would have liked to continue, because she had the feeling that online chatting with Russ could be a lot of fun, but she wasn't sure that having fun with Russ was the right thing to do.

She'd made up her mind that she didn't want to pursue a relationship with him because he was too much like Michael, and she didn't think she would survive being hurt again. At the same time, she had the impression that Russ was also pulling away — with the exception of the time she'd burst into tears and he'd held her so gently. He'd only told her what he thought she needed to hear; Marielle knew he couldn't possibly mean what he'd said. Which only proved that Michael had been right about her all along.

Now she really didn't feel like chatting.

Merrymari: I'm really wiped out and I think I'd better go to bed, it's been a long day. I'll see you tomorrow. Bye.

For a computer expert, Russ took an awfully long time to reply.

Russ999: Okay. Bye.

Tomorrow would be another day.

Marielle began at one end of the row of computers, making sure they were turned off, and Russ started at the other. They'd done it so many times, they could read each other's thoughts.

But today was different. Every time she moved on to the next computer to shut down, her heart became heavier.

Today was the last time.

The week had gone by so fast. Then on Saturday, she'd made plans with a friend just so she wouldn't have to dwell on it being the last time she'd be spending the day with him. But the whole time she was with Susan, all she could think of was Russ.

Now the church service was over, the informal Sunday youth session was over. . . .

Everything was over.

The only thing that wasn't over was the problem with Jessie and the digitally altered video.

All week long, nothing had happened. They'd waited for Jessie every night, watching in shifts, and she hadn't appeared. On the positive side, that meant nothing at the center had been disturbed — but also, nothing was resolved.

She met Russ in the middle, when the last of the computers was shut off. Marielle didn't know what to do. Did she just thank him? Tell him it had been "nice"?

He stood there and rammed his hands into his pockets. "I feel like I should say something, but my mind's gone blank."

"Same. I'm not good at goodbyes."

"This really isn't a goodbye. It's just the next stage. It's not like I won't be back. I was thinking, how about if I come back every Friday, for the later session, and on my way here from the office I'll bring pizza for everybody?"

"You don't have to do that."

"I know I don't have to. I'm offering because I want to."

While it would be nice to have him return because most of the teens would miss him, Marielle thought it would better if he came to the church services. Helping every afternoon with the teens was good for them, but going to church was good for Russ. "What about Sundays?"

"I've been considering about that. I think I'm going to go back to my own church on Sundays and catch up on everything I've missed. It's about time."

"That's great." Marielle smiled on the outside, but on the inside, she wanted to cry. Yes, she was glad he was returning to God's fold, but she wanted him to be part of God's fold in *her* church.

She had told herself that it was best to cut all ties with him. Yet she couldn't. It hurt too much.

She looked up at him. Into his beautiful brown eyes. When they first met, she'd thought his eyes were warm and friendly, and she'd been right. There was so much about him to love, she couldn't help herself. She'd fallen in love with the wrong man.

She had thought she'd been in love with Michael, but she was wrong. It was an infatuation. Michael had said and done all the right things, but that was just an image he presented to the outside world. She realized that after he treated her so cruelly.

Everything about Russ was real. She'd seen it in the way he treated others, in the way he treated her, and especially in the way he helped people when he had nothing to gain.

"Can I take you out for dinner or something?"

"I don't think that's a good idea." It was hard enough now, working up the nerve to say the official goodbye. She didn't want to do it twice. Besides, any time she spent with him from here on would be bittersweet. She needed to move forward instead of backward with her life, and strive for things she could actually attain. Russ's heart wasn't one of them. "I'm going to lock up now."

Instead of walking to the door, Russ stepped closer to her. Marielle's breath caught as he raised his hands and cupped her face. His voice dropped to a husky whisper.

"Marielle. Wait."

She could have backed away, and she knew he would have let her.

Fool that she was, she closed her eyes.

The memory of the way he had kissed her last time paled in comparison to this one. He kissed her deeply, and so tenderly that she felt herself melting in his arms. He made her feel cherished, protected and well loved.

She raised her hands to his chest and gently pushed. Everything may have been true, except the loved.

He didn't question her withdrawal, but his eyes spoke confusion, and also regret.

It took all Marielle's strength to speak. "I have to lock up. Let's go." She should have said goodbye, except that, as he'd reminded her, it wasn't really goodbye. He was coming back the following Friday, and if he kept his word, he'd be back every Friday.

She didn't know if she had the strength to deal with seeing him again, but the teens needed more help than she could give.

"I'll see you Friday," he said, and left the center.

Marielle made sure he had driven away before she finished locking the large wooden door.

The alarm went off, jolting Russ out of a too-short sleep. The red numbers on the clock radio glared 6:15 at him.

He sat up and stared at the clock as he collected his thoughts. He'd allowed himself extra time this morning, his first day back to work, because first he had to check the video taken by the webcam at the youth center. Last night's shifts at watching the youth center had been different than it had been from Monday to Saturday. Marielle's time slot hadn't changed, because she had to get up early in the morning, but when he had instant-messaged her to say he was ready to take over, she'd been uncharacteristically brief.

He'd wanted to chat. He knew that Monday morning, his life was about to change.

Sunday afternoon, as if Russ had needed the reminder, Grant had called to tell Russ that his leave was up. They needed him, and it was time to get back to work.

He sat for a while, just watching the monitor, which was trained on the empty chair.

Every other night he'd opened up a second window on his screen, even a third, and worked while keeping one eye on the webcam view.

Sunday night, he hadn't been in the mood for work because he had felt a weight bearing down on his shoulders — knowing he would be back at the office on Monday, and wouldn't be returning to the youth center until the end of the week. He would do that for a while, until the kids didn't need him anymore, and then his responsibility would end.

No ties. That was what he wanted.

Yet instead of feeling relief that it was nearly over, all he felt was regret.

After a few hours, he'd needed to sleep, he set the webcam to "video," which would record if Jessie came. Watching the clip after she'd come and gone wouldn't give him the opportunity to call the police to catch her on the premises, but it was the next best thing.

Now, Russ gathered his clothes into his arms and walked into the den, set the night's recording on fast-forward, and watched it zip by as he got dressed.

He was almost finished and was starting to put on his second sock when the camera caught the image of a person pulling out the chair to sit down.

He dropped his sock on the floor and rushed over to change the speed to real time, then watched as Jessie began the process of booting up the computer.

When the screen came up to enter the password, she gave it five or six guesses, then smacked the side of the monitor with her open hand. He saw the movement of her mouth, and he didn't want to guess what she'd said.

Suddenly, she froze.

She looked up at each of the nearby computers, then stopped and stared so openly at the webcam that it was as if she were making eye contact with Russ.

Busted.

She grabbed a piece of paper, pulled a pen out of her pocket, and wrote furiously. Then she held the paper up to the webcam.

I see you have changed your password.
I have a file in here and I want it back.
I will be in touch.

Suddenly, she was gone. The range of the

viewfinder was too limited to see where she went, and without sound, he couldn't be sure that she'd gone out through the door into the hallway, but that was what he suspected.

Russ stared at the now-lifeless monitor.

It was too late to call the police, and he knew the video from the webcam of a personal computer wouldn't be acceptable as evidence because of how easy it was to alter those types of images.

But his point had been made. Jessie knew that he knew something. He doubted she thought he'd broken into the file, but she would have figured out that he knew about it. Thus the webcam . . .

He quickly bookmarked the spot where Jessie had appeared, pulled on his second sock and rushed out the door without having breakfast.

After being off a month, he found the trip through rush-hour traffic more frustrating than he remembered. For the first time, he wondered what kind of traffic Marielle had to drive through, since she started so early, likely before the high point. His office was on the fringe of the busy downtown core because here, rent for Grant was a little cheaper. Marielle worked in the city center, in a huge high-rise tower where there was maximum exposure for a high-priced accounting firm.

He knew that once she found the time to take the courses she wanted, she would move up quickly in the hierarchy.

He arrived at his office building at the same time he always did, and walked up the stairs to his office, as he always did. Grant was there, but no one else had arrived yet.

"How was your time off? Are you feeling better and ready to get back to work?" Grant asked.

Russ's first reaction was to say that he had been ready to get back to work three weeks ago, but in fact, he'd enjoyed his time off, and if not for the pending vice presidency, he wished he could have taken more time.

"Yes, I'm ready" was all he could say.

He continued into his office, where his new computer sat ready, just waiting for him to install the programs of his choice, then transfer all the data files he'd backed up to the server.

He wasn't as excited as he thought he should be.

Instead of sitting down, Russ moved to the window. He almost expected the action would bring on a headache, but fortunately, the doctor was right. The headaches had faded, even though his memory of the accident still had not returned.

He opened the window, but he didn't lean out.

He *never* leaned out. He often stuck his head out for a breath of semi-fresh city air, grateful that the older building had windows that actually opened. But that's all he ever did. He knew accidents could happen, and he always played it safe.

He tried for only a minute to remember what might have made him lean out so far that he would fall, but then something unusual happened to Russ. His mind wandered.

Instead of wondering about his accident, he became distracted by the downtown skyline, and he thought back to all the references Marielle had made without actually giving him the address. Which of the high-rise towers was Marielle's office?

And then he wondered what she was doing.

And if she was thinking of him, too —

"Russ! Great to see you back!"

Russ spun around to see Tyler, his closest workmate, approaching, an enthusiastic smile on his face. "Hey, Tyler, it's good to see you, too. Did anybody miss me while I was gone?"

"Did we ever!" said Tyler. "Can I ask you

a question about something?"

For the rest of the morning, Russ didn't get a chance to touch his new computer. Instead, he went from desk to desk, helping everyone with problems they'd put aside in his absence.

He ordered in lunch and worked through his break so that by mid-afternoon he had his computer up and running the way he wanted it.

As soon as he had a minute alone at his computer, he checked his e-mail. Instead of starting at the top to catch up on his business correspondence, he started at the bottom, just in case Marielle had e-mailed him that morning.

Instead, there was one from Jessie, which he noted was from an untraceable source.

He opened that first.

Hi Russ,
Very clever of you with the webcam. You have seen that I have a file on your old computer that I need. This is a very treasured personal file, one I didn't want anyone to see, so I named it after Byron's account. It is imperative that I get it back immediately. It's too large a file to e-mail, and I don't want it on the company server, so I would appreciate it

if you could give me your log-in and password and I'll retrieve it myself at that old church you've been hanging around at. This means a lot to me, and your cooperation is appreciated.

Jessie

Russ read the message a second time. Now that he had discovered what was in the file, he knew what it meant to Jessie was indeed a lot — but a lot of money. He didn't want her to use the video, but since he'd added extra encryption, she could have it. Once she had it in her possession, he had no doubt that eventually she would break his code, but he wasn't going to give her that much time.

Now, all he had to do was figure out how to make sure the police would be there at the same time as Jessie. Once he gave her the password she needed, she would be gone within minutes.

He hit reply and was about to start keying, when Grant appeared in the doorway.

"I just got the strangest e-mail. I haven't heard from Jessie in a month. We've phoned and left messages, I've mailed her letters and she hasn't responded, and all my e-mails bounced back. She just quit. She said she'll forward copies of all the work

279

she's done for us that isn't finished, without charging us for it, if you'll send her a file from that project you were working on together for Byron. A number of things got held up because of Jessie disappearing. If you send her that file, and then she sends us what she's got, that would really help tie up loose ends."

"I just got an e-mail from her, too."

"Do you have that file she's talking about?"

Russ found the different story she had told Grant disturbing, but he couldn't lie. "Yes, I have it."

"Good. Send it to her right away. I need those files she's got."

"Are you sure she's really got anything? I remember the day of my accident, Jessie talked about her laptop crashing, and she said she lost everything."

Grant shrugged. "It sounds like she's got something that she didn't have backed up on our server, and it sounded important. I don't know if I trust her now after all this, but if she's got something that's more current than her backups, we need it."

Russ thought it more likely that she was simply baiting Grant, using her story for leverage to get what she wanted. Grant had no idea what was going on. Russ didn't want to tell his boss what he'd found, because so far he didn't have proof that Jessie was actually doing anything to extort Byron. So far, it was only a theory, based on Byron suddenly postponing finishing the project. That was enough for Russ to guess what was going on, but it wasn't proof.

Grant handed him a folder and left the room, allowing Russ to continue with his e-mail.

Hi Jessie,
I happen to know that your file isn't just family photos. I suggest it would be best if you don't have this file, and that I will keep it for you. Also, on the Properties function it clearly shows your name as the creator of the file, just in case you get any ideas.

Regards,
Russ

He hit Send, then opened up the folder Grant had left and was beginning to read, when the phone rang.

"Hello, Russ." The sharp tone of Jessie's voice sent a chill down Russ's spine. "I don't think you understand something. I need that file, and I need it *now.*"

"That's too bad."

"You really don't understand, do you. Do you think I can't do the same to your little church friend that I did to you?"

Russ's blood turned to ice.

"I didn't mean for you to hit the ground. I only meant for you to land on the balcony below. But I think you can see what I'm willing to do for that file. I can easily arrange an accident for your friend."

As in a nightmare, echoes of Jessie's voice calling him to the window rolled around in his head. Dizziness surged through him and he pressed one hand to the desk to support himself.

"I think you also know that I'm not working alone," she said.

The woman in the video. The man in the video whose real face had been covered. At least one of the teens at the youth center. He now didn't know if it was male or female.

"A little money goes a long way, Russ. Or a lot of money."

"You're sick."

Jessie laughed. "You're naive. I'm going to e-mail you an address, and I want you to upload my file to that server. Call the police if you want. If you do, you might get me arrested, but not for long. My friends will be watching out for me. And my friends will be watching your little friend."

Before Russ could respond, Jessie hung up.

Russ turned and stared at the window.

It hadn't been an accident.

Jessie had done something to make him fall. And if he didn't cooperate, she would hurt Marielle.

He felt like he might throw up.

On shaky legs, he walked across the office to close the door. He unclipped his cell phone from his belt and dialed Marielle's number at work.

"Hi, Marielle. Have you got a few minutes? I need something." He could have asked Grant, but he didn't want his boss. He also didn't want just a friend. He wanted Marielle.

"Sure. What do you need?"

"Jessie just phoned me, and something she said is starting to make things come back." His voice dropped to a whisper. "I need you to help me walk my way through this."

"Where are you?"

"I'm in my office." He moved across the room and opened the window. "I remember Jessie's voice calling me to the window. I'm going to lean out now."

He did so, and looked down. He didn't feel dizzy or afraid. Trying to remember

Jessie's voice, he looked down at the two-inch-wide ledge running beneath the window. "She asked me to look at the ledge. I remember that." He trained his eyes on a spot directly below the window. "It's not there now, but I remember seeing something shiny. Something gold." He squeezed his eyes shut. No headache felled him; he was thinking rationally. "A necklace. She said the clasp had broken, her necklace had fallen off and landed on the ledge, and she couldn't reach it."

He stared down at the ledge. It was a stretch, but not completely out of range.

"I'm going to reach down and see what happens."

"No! Russ! Don't!"

"I have to do this."

He reached out his arm. "I'm about eight inches short of reaching the ledge if I lean out at the waist. I'm going to put the phone down on the windowsill for a minute so I can hang on while I lean down farther, to see if I can touch it."

He balanced the phone on the edge, then spoke loudly enough for her to hear. "I'm leaning down now," he called out to the phone. "I can almost touch the ledge." He reached farther, but it wasn't enough. To give himself that extra inch, he pushed himself up on the tips of his toes, hanging on to the window frame for dear life with his left hand as he reached with his right. "I'm touching it now." As his fingers made contact, he almost felt the quick pressure of two hands from behind, and a sharp thrust.

A sensation of falling.

He remembered hitting something hard, everything spinning as he fell.

He stared at the balcony of the second-floor office, just big enough for one person to stand on, surrounded by a metal railing.

"She pushed me," he said to the phone on the sill. "I bounced off the railing at the second floor. That's how I got these cracked ribs."

The falling continued after impact. Everything turned to a cold, nondescript gray — the color of Marielle's car — and then he felt a jolt of searing pain and saw a flash of colors exploding in his head. A second jolt followed, not as extreme, and he was blinded by the glare of daylight, then everything faded to black.

That would have been when he slid off the roof of Marielle's car and landed on the hood.

He pushed himself upright now, barely able to hold on to the smooth wood edge of the sill as he steadied himself. His palms were slick with sweat, his forehead dripping, his armpits damp.

He swiped his hands on his pants and picked up the phone. "Wow. I think I need a shower. But, Marielle, I remember everything. Praise God I'm alive."

His knees began to shake, so he crossed the room and sank into his chair with a *thud.*

"Are you okay?"

Russ leaned back, letting his head fall against the high backrest. All the strength leaked out of him, leaving him completely drained. He barely had the power to raise one arm to touch the bump on his nose. It was nothing compared to what could have happened.

"Yes, I'm okay." He kept the phone pressed to his ear. It wasn't much of a connection, but it was the only connection he had. Even if all she could do was listen, he was grateful for the technology that had allowed Marielle to be with him, so he hadn't had to go through it alone.

He paused and inhaled deeply a few times, and slowly, his strength returned. "So now I know what happened. No wonder Jessie went into hiding. I could charge her with attempted murder."

"Are you going to?"

Jessie's threats of her partners doing harm

to Marielle echoed in his head. He really didn't know how far the woman would go, but what she'd done to him was far more mercenary than what he would have considered her capable of. He couldn't take the chance that Jessie and her cohorts would hurt Marielle. But he couldn't tell Marielle what Jessie had said — not until he had figured out a plan.

"I don't know yet. I have to think. It would be easy enough for her to say I just leaned too far and fell. Then it would be her word against mine."

"If she pushed you out the window to get that file, how come she didn't then get it?"

"She must not have realized that I had just started rebooting my computer when she called me to the window. After it finishes rebooting, you need to enter the password. Otherwise, she would have had it."

"Why didn't she just wait for you to leave the room? That's how she would have gotten the file on there in the first place."

"My only thought is that she needed it that same day. She probably transferred it to my computer the day before when I was out for lunch, because that's the only time I wouldn't have been in my office. I'm guessing she was going to burn it onto a DVD, but my burner is on the fritz. But the day of my accident . . ." He squeezed his eyes shut. All this time he'd been saying it was an accident, but it wasn't. He thought of what Jessie had said in their last conversation — she hadn't meant for him to hit the ground — it made sense now. Maybe she thought he would land on the balcony below, but it hadn't worked out that way. He'd hit the railing, and then continued downward to the ground below, saved only by the grace of Marielle's car being in the right place at the right time, by God's timing.

Jessie had deliberately pushed him. Maybe she hadn't meant to nearly kill him, but the fact remained that there could have been a very different ending.

"We'd been working together all day, and I guess she didn't expect me to work through lunch. After that, I wouldn't have left my office until it was time to go home. She needed at least a few minutes to find and copy that file, more time than she'd get if she just waited until my back was turned."

"Couldn't she have waited until you went to the bathroom?"

"Uh, guys don't take as long as women, Marielle. . . ."

The pause on the other end told him that she was blushing.

He smiled just thinking about it, and

found that he needed the dash of lightness for relief.

But his relief was short-lived. A *beep* signified a new e-mail, and it was a message from Jessie with the address to which he was to upload the file . . . or else . . .

"I have to go. I'll call you back."

Russ stared at Jessie's e-mail, which was only the address to the server. No text.

If he didn't upload the file, she might follow through on her threat.

He couldn't be with Marielle 24/7 to protect her, and even a restraining order wasn't a sure thing when the other party was desperate, as Jessie appeared to be.

Russ said a prayer for forgiveness and e-mailed the file to Jessie, knowing that she knew he was beaten, that he wouldn't call the police.

But he could call Marielle. And he did.

She listened quietly while he explained the whole story, and his thoughts, and his warning.

"What are you going to do?"

"There's nothing I can do. The police didn't find any fingerprints at your house after the break-in, and so they won't find any at the church, either. She was obviously smart enough to wear gloves. And just because she stuck her head out the window of my office, that isn't proof that she pushed me. Besides, you couldn't give a positive ID. I'm just assuming it was Jessie because everyone else was outside shortly after it happened, and they said she wasn't. It may be incriminating that she disappeared right at that moment, but she's a contract employee and she works her own days and hours. Also, her neighbors just think she went on vacation. When it comes down to it, it would turn into her word against ours, because we have no solid evidence for a court case. And if she didn't go to jail, the threat has been made. I can't take the risk that she'd hurt you. I have to keep quiet."

"But what about Byron? If she's blackmailing him, surely he'd be anxious to get her arrested, at least for that?"

"I haven't talked to him about it yet. He doesn't even know that I know. I can't imagine this is something he'd be anxious to share with anyone. Especially since we're only business associates."

"But you have to tell Byron that you know about what she's doing, and that you know it's a fabrication. Then whatever Jessie does won't matter."

"I can't be sure of that. What if Jessie still gives the video to Byron's wife? That video is so well done that I wouldn't have been able to tell it was a fabrication if I hadn't paused it and analyzed the pixel coloring. But even if Byron's wife did believe him, that would increase the reason for Jessie to retaliate. She'd go to jail for that, but they don't keep a person in jail forever, even for extortion and attempted murder. You'd never be safe. So my answer is no, I'm not telling him anything. I need more time."

"That's it?"

"Yes. I know it will cost Byron a lot of money, but it's only money. You're safe, his marriage is safe, and that's where it's got to stay. I have to get back to work now, I have a lot to do. I'll see you Friday evening. Goodbye, Marielle."

CHAPTER SEVENTEEN

Marielle stared at the phone.

Jessie had almost killed Russ, and it wasn't even a crime of hatred. Jessie did it simply to get him out of the way.

Marielle couldn't imagine a person so cold and heartless that they would do such a thing, but yet the world was full of such evil. Never in her worst dreams would she have imagined something like this could happen to someone she knew.

And he wasn't going to do anything about it out of concern for her, and for Byron's marriage.

It's only money.

She could barely believe he'd said that. While Russ had more than enough money to make ends meet now, he had known a time when he didn't have enough money to live. His family had only survived through charity, and by a debt that took Russ ten years of his life to pay off.

Usually people who said "only" in front of the word *money* had never known what it was like not to have any. As the saying went, Money can't buy love, but love doesn't pay the rent.

And this wasn't only about money. It was extortion, it was illegal, and it would also be never-ending.

A threat had been made, and she admired Russ's decision to protect her, and to protect his client's marriage. But this time, it wasn't Russ's decision to make. The threat had been made against Marielle, and therefore, it was her decision.

Marielle walked into the kitchen and pulled Russ's flash drive out from under one of the cups in the back of the cupboard. She wasn't going to watch the sickening video, even though she knew it was fake. What she was going to obtain was far more important than that.

She plugged it into her computer, opened the window and read the name of the file — which was the name of the company. Then she called up the company's Web site and went to the page listing the board of directors. She remembered hearing the man's first name, so she scrolled down the list to find his full name and direct line.

Marielle took a few seconds to pray for

wisdom, and dialed. A man answered.

"Am I speaking to Byron Tanner?"

"This is Byron Tanner."

"You don't know me. My name is Marielle McGee and I'm a friend of Russ Branson."

Byron paused. "Yes?"

Marielle thought the hesitation in his voice was understandable. "I'm calling to tell you that Russ and I know about the video Jessie made, and we know it's a fabrication."

The line remained silent, which Marielle had expected, so she gave Byron time to think.

"Go ahead," he finally said.

Marielle started at the beginning, explaining how they found the file, how Russ discovered it was altered, and how they figured out that Jessie was using it to extort money out of him, which he agreed was correct. "I know you think you're protecting your wife, but that might be only short term. I also have to admit that I have ulterior motives for calling." Marielle paused to take a deep breath. "I was once engaged, and my fiancé was cheating on me. As is typical, I was the last to know. I know people were talking about me behind my back, and it hurt. It still hurts that no one told me. I also still feel the hurt of the betrayal. The reason I wanted to tell you this personally, beyond the issue with the money and how wrong this is, is that I don't want someone else to suffer the way I did. Do you know what I mean?"

"Yes, I think so . . ."

"If Jessie goes forward with this, even though it's a complete scam, it would hurt your wife deeply. There's also the trust. Once the seed has been planted, doubts are impossible to erase."

"Why are you telling me this?"

"Because I'm trying to say, don't take the chance that someone else will tell her or show her the video. Don't wait for the day it becomes an issue. Tell her yourself, and tell her now. If you want, I can be there, or you can have her call me to verify that this is the truth. I'll testify in court for you, too, if you want me to."

There was silence for a moment on the line.

"I need time to think about what you've said," said Byron. "Thank you for telling me. It actually feels good to have someone say that, and know it isn't true. I'll probably be in touch with you."

Marielle gave Byron her office number, her home number and her cell number, and then left for the youth center.

When she arrived, there was another

vehicle in the parking lot, but it wasn't Russ's SUV. It was a news van, complete with a photographer and a reporter.

The reporter held a microphone in her face. "Are you Marielle McGee, the person who runs this program?"

"Uh . . . Yes . . ."

"I've been assigned to run a human interest segment on inner-city youth organizations, and I remembered that an accident down there last month led to your group receiving a donation of computers and tutoring from an employee of the company that made the donations. Would you mind if I asked you a few questions and we took some pictures?"

"First I have to ask the participants if they're okay with having their pictures taken."

The reporter smiled. "Don't worry. It's standard procedure for us to have them sign waivers, and if any of them are underage, we ask them to have their parents or legal guardian sign a waiver before we go to print."

"Okay, in that case, ask me anything you want."

Marielle leaned closer to the washroom mirror and added a touch of blush to her cheeks and returned to the youth center room.

Brittany rushed to her side. "Russ is coming, isn't he?"

"Yes. Did you see our pictures in the paper this morning?" asked Marielle.

Brittany nodded so fast her hair bounced. "Yes. Is what the article said true?"

Marielle led Brittany to the desk. "It sure is. But let's talk about that when Russ gets here. I bought a whole pile of newspapers this morning, and I cut out and laminated a copy of the picture and the article for everyone in it. Would you like to help me hand them out?" The teens were gathered and waiting expectantly.

As Brittany identified everyone in the photo and gave the copies out, Marielle watched her pile disappear. It had cost to get all the laminating done, but the photo of everyone together as a happy group was just too good not to save. For most of the teens, having their picture in the newspaper would be a once-in-a-lifetime event. Marielle wanted them all to have a memento of this group for when they got older, hopefully to keep them motivated in striving for the best life had to offer.

When Russ's SUV pulled into the parking lot, all the chatter died to a silence. The second the door opened and Russ stepped inside the building, cheers erupted.

He grinned from ear to ear. "I see you all read the paper."

The group cheered again.

Marielle quickly stepped up to him and shooed everyone else away. "Did you read about the funding?"

Russ nodded. "Yes. Did you find out how much your group is getting?"

"No, but it doesn't matter how much. Anything is better than nothing."

"Agreed. Now I have some great news for you."

"I can hardly wait."

"Grant gave me the promotion. All the publicity has already made a difference, in just one day, but he said he was planning on giving it to me anyway. So you're now looking at the new vice president."

Marielle grasped his hands. "That's wonderful! Tell me, what's the first thing you're going to do?"

Russ's smile widened. "Put my house up for sale."

Marielle dropped his hands. "Pardon me?"

"My first assignment is to open up a new branch, and that means moving."

"Moving? Where?"

"Across the state."

"Did you know about this? Is this what you wanted?"

"Yes, this is exactly what I wanted. I've been working toward this for years. I can hardly believe it's finally happened."

Marielle forced herself to smile, but she had a feeling it looked as phony as it felt. "Then I'm happy for you."

"After we wind everything up tonight, would you like to go out and celebrate with me? It can be the first entry on my new expense account."

Celebrating was the last thing she felt like doing. Yet, she'd known all along that he'd been striving for a promotion to kick his career up to the next level. She just hadn't thought it would involve losing him. Not that she had ever had him.

"I'm not sure. Maybe —"

The ring tone of Russ's cell phone cut off her words, which was a profound relief.

He checked the display, then held the phone to his ear.

"Hi, Byron! What can I do for you?"

Suddenly, he smiled. "That's great! Just give me a call when you're ready, and I'll do everything I can to get you back on schedule."

Russ flicked the phone shut. "That was Byron. He says he's ready to get going again with his project. It was nearly finished when he shut it down."

Marielle nodded. "That's good news. I hope he can —"

This time, Marielle's cell phone rang.

She checked the display and didn't recognize the number, but she flicked the phone open and answered it anyway.

"Hi, Marielle. This is Byron Tanner. We spoke the other day."

"Yes. Of course. I remember talking to you. How's it going?" Marielle listened, nodding and muttering her agreement as Byron relayed his story — and how everything was okay with his wife.

"That's great! You've very welcome. I'm glad it all worked out."

She closed the phone and tucked it back in her pocket. "That was Byron. He says he talked to his wife about what's been happening. Apparently he was putting the money through his business, paying Jessie out as contract labor so his wife wouldn't see what was happening — and it was putting his company in financial difficulty. He informed the bank, and thanks to a very alert clerk, the police were called when Jessie was in the process of cashing a check. They traced the money that's been going out of the account, and arrested three more people, one of them a juvenile who is already known to the police. He's not a member of your group, so that's a relief!"

"I figured as much, and it looks like I was right, because he wants to . . ." Russ's voice trailed off. "Wait just a minute. Why did he call you to tell you this?"

Marielle gulped. "After you and I talked, I phoned Byron and told him that we knew what was going on, and that we would stand up for him either to his wife, or in court."

Russ crossed his arms over his chest. "I thought we agreed that you were going to drop it."

"*I* didn't say that. *You* said that. Since you were so worried about me, I took the initiative and called Byron, so if anything happened, you wouldn't blame yourself."

"You shouldn't have taken that risk."

"It was something I had to do. I couldn't let it continue, for his sake, for his wife's sake, and for ours. Wrong is wrong, Russ. But it's okay now. Everyone has been arrested, so there's no one left to carry out her threats. I would think the police should be calling you soon to ask if you'll press charges for attempted murder."

"I didn't want you to get involved in this."

"I was involved whether I wanted to be or not. How do you think it was going to get

301

solved?"

Russ stiffened. "I was going to talk to Byron's wife, and at the same time, I was going to mention the threats Jessie made about you. I'm guessing you missed that little detail when you talked to Byron, didn't you?" Russ said.

"Of course I didn't tell him. If I had told him, I don't know if he would have talked to his wife or dealt with it so quickly. Maybe he would have tried to do something stupid himself. It's just that there is so much money involved. I don't know. I think this was a good solution. And now it's over." Marielle sighed.

"Don't you understand? Your *life* could have been over! How could you be so irresponsible?"

"Me?" Marielle pressed one palm over her heart. "You're the one who was going to let it go."

"I wasn't going to let it go!" He waved a hand in the air. "I was trying to figure out what to do! I couldn't take the risk that she would have done to you what she did to me. I would have figured something out — I just needed a little time."

"Then I saved you the trouble. The whole group is under arrest. I don't understand why you're so angry."

302

"I'm angry because . . ." Russ cut off his own words and gritted his teeth. "I'm just angry, okay!"

"Will you quit shouting? Everyone is starting to stare."

He froze, and his arms dropped to his sides. "This isn't going to work. I think I should go home. I have to pack and leave first thing in the morning, anyway. I'll see you around."

Before she could respond, he spun on his heel and stormed out of the center.

Brittany appeared at her side. "He sure seems mad."

"He's not mad. He's angry."

"Whatever. He's leaving. Aren't you going to go after him?"

Marielle watched through the window as his taillights disappeared around the corner.

He'd told her honestly from the beginning what he wanted, and it wasn't her. She had no right to be disappointed, no right to feel hurt.

But she couldn't help it. A part of her had been ripped away. Losing him was going to leave a huge, aching hole in her heart for the rest of her life.

But this was his choice, and he'd never lied or misled her. This was what he wanted, and she wasn't going to try to pull it away from him.

She loved him too much to do that.

"No, Brittany. I'm not."

Chapter Eighteen

"That last one looked real good. I'll be in touch."

The real estate agent smiled, pumped his hand, gave him a business card and left, not a moment too soon for Russ.

He closed the hotel door behind him and walked to the glass patio door at the back of the room.

He just had a few things to finish up. He'd done it.

His house was up for sale, and here he was, looking over the skyline of the city that would be his new home. And he was about to make an offer on a new executive-style house, the kind he'd dreamed of all his life. A large double garage, hot tub, sauna and even a huge exercise room in the basement. It was everything a man could ask for.

God had truly blessed him. He was on the edge of a new beginning, about to have everything he'd ever worked and strived for.

All his friends were happy for him. His mother and his sister were ecstatic.

But yet, he felt no joy in his achievements.

Marielle wasn't here with him. Right now she would be sitting in her living room, sipping a cup of tea, winding down for the night.

He wondered if she was as miserable as he was.

Except that how he felt was his own fault.

He slid the patio door open and stepped out on the balcony. The brisk, fresh wind rippled his hair and cooled his skin.

It was beautiful here. The mountains rose in the distance, and the air was fresh and clean. On the flight in, just before they landed they'd gone over a large park with a lake in the center.

He couldn't get his mind off that park. When he was a young boy there had been a small pond in a vacant corner of the lot behind their apartment building. Actually, it had been more of a permanent puddle in the middle of a patch of wild bushes, fed by the ditch when it overflowed after a heavy rain. One wild duck had called it home for a while, and that was enough for Russ to have considered it a pond. It wasn't much, but he'd spent much time there as a boy. It became a place where he could hide to escape the pressures of the city and all the things that weighed him down, even temporarily.

He didn't know why, but as soon as he had picked up the rented car, instead of going to the office building Grant had told him to look at, Russ had driven the long way, to the park. As soon as he'd stepped out of the car, he knew he'd found another special place to go when he needed some quiet time. The sky was bright and clear, and only a hint of a breeze rippled the water. It was peaceful and serene, and perfect, a place he could rest his weary soul.

The real estate agent had even found him a house close enough that Russ could walk there in just a few minutes. But . . .

He didn't have anyone to share it with.

Was this really what he wanted and what he'd worked so hard to become?

Russ rested his hands on the railing to lean on it, and stared over the expanse of the darkening sky. Lights of the city began to wink on below him. For the first time in his life he'd felt happy when working with Marielle and her ragtag group of underprivileged youths. He'd done his best to help the kids to avoid many of the struggles he'd had to go through, and it had felt good.

But more than missing being with the kids

at the center, Russ missed Marielle.

He didn't just miss her. He loved her. He'd almost told her so last night, but he hadn't wanted to shout it at her in anger. Except now, in hindsight, he realized that meant he hadn't told her at all.

He leaned on the balcony railing, squeezed his eyes shut and lifted his face to the cool breeze.

In his mind's eye, he pictured the park and imagined it wasn't the updraft from the city street below, but the tangy air off the lake that was teasing his hair and cheeks.

Better than just being in the park would be being in the park with Marielle, experiencing it with her.

The picture of the two of them together formed in his mind, almost as real as if it were actually happening. He visualized her wearing the same dress she'd worn to church last Sunday, a loose pale thing that was both comfortable and practical, typical of Marielle. He imagined them together, laughing as they kicked off their shoes. He could almost hear Marielle's voice as she told him to roll up his pants so he wouldn't get them dirty, and then when his handiwork met her satisfaction, they would begin their journey around the calm lake. He could almost feel the wet sand between his toes as they would walk together, side by side. A lone bird would be singing in the tree, serenading them. They wouldn't have to speak, the beauty of the moment would eliminate the need for words. She would smile, not at anything in particular he'd said, but just from the joy of being together, uninterrupted, with nothing to pressure them to hurry or leave such a beautiful place.

His heart quickened at the thought.

Of course, he'd smile back, and then he'd reach out to hold her hand. He could imagine her looking up into his eyes, the breeze off the lake lifting her hair, teasing the red stripe, just as he'd done not long ago.

They would stop walking and look deeply into each others' eyes.

He would drop his shoes and hold her waist, and she would do the same to him.

Then he'd lower his head to kiss her, sweetly, the way he should have done before he went to the airport.

A siren echoed up from the street.

The picture in his mind faded to gray, as quickly as a scene changing in a movie.

Russ opened his eyes and stared blankly out into the cityscape, darker now.

The lights and movement below no longer

held the same appeal. Instead of the activity of the city below offering promise, it only reminded him of where he was, which wasn't the place he'd been calling home.

He turned and walked back inside the hotel room, professionally decorated and full of fine furnishings, and turned around to shut the balcony door behind him. As he slid the door closed, he saw the reflection of a well-dressed man in a tailored suit, surrounded by all the trappings of success, looking back at him.

A man who was all alone.

Russ stared at his reflection. The victory was hollow.

The Lord God said, "It is not good for the man to be alone. I will make a helper suitable for him." Genesis 2:18

Marielle was more than just "suitable" for him. She was all he'd ever wanted, and all he'd ever need. She was perfect for him. He'd felt it from the first time he met her, even though he hadn't realized it at the time. First he'd fallen head first out his office window, and then he'd fallen head over heels in love with Marielle.

And now he was tossing her aside for a cold, sterile existence, looking down at the world instead of living in it, with Marielle at his side.

Russ walked to the desk at the far side of the room, hit the autodial on the phone and called for a cab. Wasting no time, he sat down on one end of the bed and, using the remote control, punched in all that was needed to check out. Then he picked up his suitcase, still unopened, and left the room.

The cab was ready and waiting for him in the street. At the airport he had to wait for the second flight, but he caught the red-eye on standby, and was on his way home.

Home.

To Marielle.

It was three in the morning by the time he finally pulled up to his house, but he didn't go inside. He walked straight from the cab to the For Sale sign in the middle of his front yard, and not caring that he was wearing his most expensive suit, he pulled the sign up and threw it beside the house where no one could see it.

He didn't even bother to put his suitcase in the house. He tossed it in the back seat of his SUV, fired up the engine and roared off to Marielle's town house.

All the lights were out, as were her neighbors'. Russ rang the doorbell, then rang it again when she didn't come down within a minute. He waited another thirty seconds, then knocked on the door, trying hard not to pound in his urgency.

The door creaked open. Marielle appeared on the threshold, wrapped in a fuzzy housecoat that had seen better days and wearing big fat bunny slippers on her feet. Her hair was a disaster, sticking out at all angles, and the remains of the previous day's makeup was smudged down her cheeks.

She was a mess, but she was the most beautiful thing he'd ever seen.

"Russ? What are you doing here?"

"I was thinking. With all the technology available, I don't really have to move. I can do everything remotely from my desk, and travel when there's something that has to be handled in person."

She blinked and stared up at him. "You came here in the middle of the night to tell me that? What time is it?"

Russ didn't have to check his watch. He knew what time it was because he'd looked only a few seconds before she opened the door. "It's 3:27 a.m."

Her eyes widened and she looked past him, to his SUV parked on the street. "Why are you wearing your good suit? What's wrong?"

"What's wrong is my job. I don't need to move. If Grant really wants to have someone live out there and start up a new office, he can pick someone else. I'm staying here."

She gulped. "Wh-why?" she stammered.

He stepped closer to her and lifted one hand slowly to rest his fingers on her cheek. "Because I love you," he said softly, then smiled. "I came back because I should have said it before I left. I love you, Marielle, and I'm asking if you will do me the honor of becoming my wife."

"Your wife? You came here in the middle of the night to propose to me?" She stared at his suit and tie, which he knew bore streaks of mud from pulling out the For Sale sign, but he didn't care. That's what dry cleaners were for.

"Yes, I did. Do you have an answer for me? It's a yes-or-no kind of question, and I'm hoping that you'll say yes."

Marielle stepped back. "I look horrible. I'm a mess." She pressed both hands over her mouth. "I haven't brushed my teeth."

"I can't tell if that's a yes or a no."

"But I'm in my housecoat and slippers. I look awful."

"You don't look awful. Even if you did, I'd love you anyway. But you look kinda cute in that big floppy housecoat, actually. Like you should be snuggling a baby in your arms right now."

"C-cute . . . ? B-baby . . . ?"

"Do you want children? I'd like children. I promise you that I'm not going to take off at the first hint of trouble or if times get rough. I'm in for the long haul."

"Are you sure about this?"

"I've never been more sure of anything in my life. Just to let you know, I don't expect you to pack up and move to be with me. I grew up without anyone besides my mother and my sister, no extended family, no roots. You've got roots here, and I'm not going to pull you away from this. I've been working hard all my life, but I just figured out that it wasn't money or a secure job that I wanted. It's the security a good job can bring. And all that security means nothing if I don't have you. I'm happy where I am, at my job in my office in that little old building, and helping out with your 'kids,' and mostly, I'm happy when I'm with you. I'm staying, and if that's not good enough for Grant, I don't want to start from the bottom in a new job again, but I've done it before. I can do it again. By the way, I hope you don't mind a short engagement."

"You're serious, aren't you?"

"Yup." He reached out and clasped her delicate hands in his. "I love you, Marielle, but I haven't heard that you love me, and you haven't answered my question. I'm starting to feel more than a little insecure right now."

Her eyes grew bright, and he didn't think it was the reflection of the street lamp behind him.

"Of course I love you. How could I not love you? I love you so much that I'd marry you anywhere you wanted to go, whether it's here, or if you have to move to the ends of the earth."

Russ felt like his heart was going to burst. He wanted to sing and dance and tell the world, except the world was sleeping. At least their part of the world was, except for him and Marielle.

"I should go. We both have to get up for work in the morning. We've both got to get to bed."

"You think I'm going to be able to sleep now?"

"No. But you should try. I'll sneak off a bit early and see you at the youth center tomorrow."

She backed up inside but didn't close the door. "Okay. I love you, Russ."

He smiled. "I love you, too, and good night."

Dear Reader,

In the poem *The Road Not Taken* by Robert Frost, the speaker came to a crossroad in his life, and knowing he could never go back in time to this exact same place, he stopped to think on his choices, made a decision and then took the road "less traveled by."

In Russ's life, falling out the window and landing on Marielle's car was definitely something that started a chain of life-changing events, but it didn't really change his life at that moment. After he healed, he simply went back to work, hopefully a better person, but nothing was different except for the bump on his nose. The change happened when, according to his hopes and dreams, and in the culmination of years of hard work, he reached the top, looked out to see his future and then decided that really wasn't what was best for him, God had something else in mind for him. He then took the more difficult path back home to Marielle.

Everyone at some point in their lives will have at least one monumental decision to make — something that will change the path of their lives forever. I hope that when we all come to that choice, we will stop, like Russ, think, lean on God for His help, trust — and then not be afraid to take the right path, even if it is the one "less traveled by."

God bless you in your journeys!

Gail Sattler

QUESTIONS FOR DISCUSSION

1. At the beginning of the book, Marielle pulled off the road and out of traffic in order to answer her cell phone. Do you know anyone who has had an accident or a near-miss because of answering the phone while driving? What happened, why do you think it happened and what could have been done to prevent it?

2. It was quite a shock for Marielle to have a person land on her car. It can be difficult to maintain a clear head and do what is best in that type of situation. If the same thing happened to you, what would you do? What would be your best advice to someone else in the same situation?

3. Marielle worked hard to develop a relationship with the teens, and to some, her only ministry could be that she was a

good example of a Christian. If someone was watching you, would you be a good example? What is it you do that could be a good example to someone else? If you were trying hard to be a good example, who would be watching?

4. Who do you know that shines as a good example? What is it that they did that made them shine? How can you follow their example in your own life?

5. Marielle helped with the preschool-level Sunday school. Have you ever participated in a group leading children? What was your biggest challenge?

6. Russ's time to work at the youth center is limited. Have you ever been involved in a short-term project? How did you feel when your time was coming to an end?

7. Jessie had broken into both Russ's and Marielle's homes. Have you ever been the victim of a home invasion? How did that make you feel? What did you do after the invasion? What did you do to make sure it wouldn't happen again? Or, if it does happen again, what would you have

done to be prepared?

8. Once Russ became aware of what Jessie was doing, he made a plan to catch her in the act of breaking in. Do you think he did the right thing? Why or why not?

9. After Russ and Marielle discussed what Jessie was doing to Byron, Russ's client, they had different opinions of what to do, and when. What would you have done? What would you like others to do, if the same thing were happening to you?

10. In the end, Russ potentially left his career hanging and flew back to Marielle in the middle of the night. How did you feel about his decision and the actions he took to be with her again?

ABOUT THE AUTHOR

Gail Sattler lives in Vancouver, British Columbia (where you don't have to shovel rain), with her husband of twenty-seven years, three sons, two dogs, five lizards, one toad and a degu named Bess. Gail loves to read stories with a happy ending, which is why she writes them. Visit Gail's Web site at www.gailsattler.com

The employees of Thorndike Press hope you have enjoyed this Large Print book. All our Thorndike and Wheeler Large Print titles are designed for easy reading, and all our books are made to last. Other Thorndike Press Large Print books are available at your library, through selected bookstores, or directly from us.

For information about titles, please call:
   (800) 223-1244

or visit our Web site at:
   www.gale.com/thorndike
   www.gale.com/wheeler

To share your comments, please write:
   Publisher
   Thorndike Press
   295 Kennedy Memorial Drive
   Waterville, ME 04901